William E. Norris

A Victim of Good Luck

A novel

William E. Norris

A Victim of Good Luck
A novel

ISBN/EAN: 9783337046040

Printed in Europe, USA, Canada, Australia, Japan

Cover: Foto ©Andreas Hilbeck / pixelio.de

More available books at **www.hansebooks.com**

A VICTIM OF GOOD LUCK

A

VICTIM OF GOOD LUCK

A NOVEL

W. E. NORRIS

AUTHOR OF "THE COUNTESS RADNA," ETC.

IN TWO VOLUMES

VOL. I.

LONDON
WILLIAM HEINEMANN
1894

CONTENTS OF VOL. I.

CHAPTER   PAGE

    I. THE RECTOR OF HARBURY VALE   -   -   1

   II. VERONICA   -   -   -   -   -   17

  III. THE PREACHER AND THE POET   -   -   32

  IV. VERONICA MAKES INQUIRIES -   -   -   48

   V. THE INJURED INNOCENT   -   -   -   62

  VI. A FRIENDLY COMPACT   -   -   -   80

 VII. DOLLY CRADOCK   -   -   -   -   94

VIII. COMPLICATIONS   -   -   -   -   111

  IX. VERONICA IS HIGHLY COMPLIMENTED -   -   125

   X. AN INCOMPLETE EXPLANATION   -   -   141

  XI. ENOUGH OF IT   -   -   -   -   155

 XII. HORACE CUTS A POOR FIGURE   -   -   169

XIII. THE NEW ORDER OF THINGS -   -   -   186

VICTIM OF GOOD LUCK

CHAPTER I.

THE RECTOR OF HARBURY VALE.

THE Reverend John Dimsdale was seated in his study, one fine spring morning, wrestling with the composition of a discourse, to be delivered on the coming Sunday. Although he had for many years been in the habit of preaching without notes, it was, nevertheless, necessary that his sermons should be well thought out in advance, and he had not found that any great economy of time was effected by the abandonment of pen and paper. For he was a nervous, conscientious, irritable man—as anybody might have discovered by a glance at his high, wrinkled forehead, his bald head, his twitching lips and the long thin fingers, which kept plucking his gray beard

—and he always tried hard not to scamp his work, distasteful as a large portion of it was to him. At Harbury Vale, of which country parish in the Thames valley he had been rector for so long that he had quite ceased to dream of possible preferment, he was accounted a very fine preacher, and people who came from as far off as Windsor and Reading on purpose to hear him seldom went away disappointed. Probably not one in a hundred guessed how much he hated preaching. Fluency, and even occasional eloquence, he ought to have known that he possessed; but, as a matter of fact, he could not feel sure of himself. Like those self-distrustful persons who have escaped sea-sickness through a score of voyages, yet who never set foot on shipboard without an inward sinking of the heart, he had no confidence in his own invincibility, and the possibility of a disastrous breakdown was always before his eyes.

On this particular morning he was more than usually worried. " Set your affections on things above, not on things of the earth " was to be the theme of his homily, and he was conscious of being altogether out of harmony with it. The principle, of course, was sound, and might be supported by the customary commonplace reflections, but poor

Mr. Dimsdale did not want to be more common-place than he could help, and he had not, so far, been able to see his way to any original utterances. He pushed his chair back from the table, got up and began to pace restlessly about the room, rumpling his sparse hair with both hands.

"'Fret not thyself, and verily thou shalt be fed' . . . Oh, dear! what dreadful nonsense that sounds! As if any man was likely to get bread and butter unless he fretted himself . . . or even if he did! Well, there's something in that. It isn't the fretting that earns the bread and butter—it's the quiet, persistent performance of daily duties. At any rate, one might be justified in saying so, though it does seem to me that a man may perform his daily duties in a quiet, persistent way for a great number of years and yet not know where to turn for a five-pound note at the end of them. 'The world is too much with us' . . . Yes, but that isn't always our fault. Troubles come, emergencies arise, and we have to deal with them; it's monstrous to tell an unfortunate fellow that he ought to have faith and believe that all is ordered for the best. Your daughters marry poor curates and have babies every year, and if you don't help them out, nobody will;

your only son gets plucked for the army, and seems to think it rather a good joke than otherwise. It is as much as you can do to pay the weekly bills . . . and upon the top of all that, you must needs exhort your fellow-sufferers to take no heed for the morrow !"

The Rector walked to the window and rested his burning forehead upon the glass. Outside, the sun was shining brightly upon the lawn, upon the yellow crocuses and the Lent-lilies ; a missel-thrush, perched upon a bare bough, was singing exultant defiance to the east wind ; the horse-chestnut buds were bursting. It would have been pleasant to go out for a walk and get rid of the cobwebs, but that was not to be thought of. Work must be done first, and there was not too much time left to do it in. Naturally, therefore, the slow creak of the opening door was a sound to be resented.

It was Mrs. Dimsdale, who, with a copy of the *Times* in her hand, had come in to say, " What do you think, John ? Old Mr. Trevor is dead."

" Well, my dear," the Rector returned rather crossly, " really I can't help it if he is. *I* didn't kill him."

Mrs. Dimsdale seated herself in one of the worn,

leather-covered arm-chairs and laughed. She was a stout, comfortable-looking matron, who had had her share of good looks in days gone by, and whose rounded cheeks were not disfigured by the lines with which care had furrowed those of her husband.

"But it's most interesting, you know," she protested. "Are you still up in the clouds, John? Have you forgotten who Mr. Trevor was?"

"I have not forgotten, nor am I likely to forget," answered the Rector, "what a thorn Mr. Trevor has been in the side of his bishop and of the Church. I believe him to have been honest, though bigoted and mischievous. At the same time, Elizabeth, I must ask you to postpone all discussion of his merits or demerits to some other occasion. I have my sermon to think out, and——"

"Sit down, John, and don't get into a state of mind. You know how useless it is for you to rehearse sermons when you are not in the temper for them. I can see by your face that you have come to a knot; and at such moments there is only one thing to be done—drop the subject. I am very sorry I didn't interrupt you sooner. Now I am going to read you what the *Times* says about Mr. Trevor. It is under the heading of 'Obituary,' and they have given him three-quarters of a column all to himself."

The Rector, who had long since acquired the experience which every married man ends by acquiring, sat down and folded his hands patiently, while his wife, after adjusting her spectacles, proceeded to quote the following appreciative paragraph—

" ' The religious and charitable world may be said to have sustained a severe loss by the death of Mr. Trevor, J.P. and D.L., who passed away yesterday at his residence, Broxham Hall, Norfolk, in a green old age. Although the deceased gentleman took no active part in politics after the passing of the Reform Act of 1868, and resigned his seat in Parliament immediately upon the enactment of a measure to which he was strongly opposed, his name and his person have not ceased throughout the last quarter of a century to be familiar to his fellow-countrymen. Whether the frequent prosecutions with which his memory will be identified were or were not ill-advised, whether his outspoken hatred of Ritualism and his dread of the foothold obtained in England during his lifetime by the Church of Rome were exaggerated or not, are questions which are scarcely

likely to be answered in the sense that he would
have wished by a generation which has grown tolerant,
if not indifferent, as to such matters; but it will be
conceded alike by friend and foe that Samuel Trevor
was a man of the strictest integrity and the most
blameless personal life.   Born as long ago as 1807,
and educated in the tenets of the Evangelical school,
to which his father, a well-known politician of the
day, belonged, Samuel Trevor imbibed, while still a
young man, principles from which he never swerved
until the last day of his life.'

"Then," said Mrs. Dimsdale, looking up over her
spectacles, "there is a great deal about Wilberforce
and Buxton and Clapham, and all that sort of thing.
Also about his prosecutions of the Ritualists and the
money that he spent upon them, and so forth.   You
can read it to yourself afterwards, if you like."

"I don't think I particularly care to read it,"
answered the Rector of Harbury Vale, who was a
moderate High Churchman.

"No; I dare say not.   Well, here is the finish of
it. 'But when all is said and done, the claims which
the late Mr. Trevor possessed upon public esteem
and veneration are beyond dispute.   Vehement and
occasionally bitter as a controversialist he may have

been; his methods of testifying to the sincerity of
his religious convictions may not always have
commended themselves to modern approval; but
his boundless generosity, his unfailing care for the
sick and needy and the admirable uses to which he
devoted a large fortune, of which more than half is
said to have been expended by him upon good
works, will, it is to be hoped, be remembered long
after the somewhat vexatious proceedings which he
deemed it his duty, of recent years, to institute
against offending clergymen have been forgotten
and forgiven.' Dear me, what a prodigious sentence! I only saw him once. He struck me as
being a particularly disagreeable old man."

"H'm! He struck a good many other people in
the same light, my dear," observed the Rector,
stroking his beard meditatively. "I wonder whether
he has done anything for Veronica."

"Why, of course he has!" returned Mrs. Dimsdale, with a touch of impatience. "That's just it;
that's why I say that his death is an interesting
event. He promised to provide for her, you know."

"I think not, Elizabeth; I certainly did not understand that there had been any definite promise.
Some years ago, when Mrs. Mansfield endeavoured

unsuccessfully to arrange a meeting between him and his niece, he did, I believe, say that her name would probably be found in his will; but that was all. And very little, I should think, can be expected from such a rancorous old—ahem!—from so obstinately prejudiced a person as he was."

"Ah! you are such a pessimist, John! I don't mean about Mr. Trevor's character, because I quite agree with you that he was an unnatural old horror, but about Veronica's prospects. After all, she is his sister's only child."

"As he refused to hold any communication with his sister after her marriage, and as he could never be persuaded to see her only child, that seems rather a poor foundation to build Spanish castles upon," remarked the Rector dryly. "May I ask, Elizabeth, whether you expect to hear that he has constituted Veronica his sole heiress?"

"No, John, I do not; but I expect to hear that he has left her something like £10,000—I don't mind telling you that."

"I trust you will not be foolish enough to tell the girl anything so absurd. You will only lay up an utterly unnecessary disappointment for her if you do."

"I doubt whether any disappointment of that kind would affect her; Veronica cares so little about money, poor dear! But I am convinced that she will inherit a handsome sum; and so would you be, John, if you were not determined to see everything *en noir* this morning."

"If I saw the world through rose-coloured glasses just at present I should possess your highly enviable temperament, my dear, and Heaven has not so far favoured me. It is all very fine to be cheerful and sanguine, but one must have some sort of reasonable ground for feeling so, or at least so it appears to me. I know I ought to send poor Lizzie a trifle, and Martha writes to say that they have decided to put down the pony-cart, though how they are to manage without a conveyance of some kind in that lonely parish I'm sure I don't know. And here is Joe upon one's hands, and likely to remain upon one's hands indefinitely."

"Don't trouble about Joe," said Mrs. Dimsdale placidly. "With his talents he is certain to make his way in the world sooner or later, and I don't know that his having failed for the army is such a great misfortune, after all. A military career has so very few prizes to offer."

" And, such as they are, it would have been very strange if he had secured one of them. There I am quite with you, Elizabeth. However great Joe's talents may be, they have never yet enabled him to carry off a prize of any description—not even a good-conduct prize."

" Well, John," returned Mrs. Dimsdale, bristling up, as she always did when any of her offspring were attacked, " I really don't think that you have had any cause to complain of Joe's conduct, at all events. And you yourself have always admitted that he has twice as much intelligence as the generality of boys and young men."

" Oh, he has intelligence, he has plenty of intelligence—coupled with eccentricity. Whether that combination is likely to be of any practical service to him is another question. For nothing can be more certain than that he will have to earn his daily bread somehow or other. I am not Mr. Trevor, remember; I am neither as rich nor as robust as he was; and when I die there will be little enough left for those whom I am bound to provide for to live upon."

" It will all come right, John," Mrs. Dimsdale declared soothingly; " and even if it were all going to come wrong, suffering in anticipation would not mend matters.   The truth is that you want a tonic."

" No, no !" returned the Rector hastily—for he had had ample experience of his wife's doses, and he knew what the effects of them generally were— " I assure you I don't want that, my dear.   What I really do want is to be permitted to get on with my sermon, for which you have already furnished me with some valuable hints.   One should strive to cultivate your habitual frame of mind ; one should never suffer in anticipation.   I am convinced of it, and I will tell the people so."

Mrs. Dimsdale rose slowly, picked up her newspaper and moved towards the door.   " I only wish you would practise what you preach !" she remarked.   " Then you wouldn't give yourself a headache by struggling with ideas which would come quite naturally to you if you waited for them until you were in the pulpit.   I must try to find Veronica now and tell her the news."

The Rector, who had drawn his chair up to the writing-table once more, looked over his shoulder to say, " For goodness' sake, don't go and tell her that she has come into a fortune !"

" Of course I shall do nothing of the kind,"

answered Mrs. Dimsdale; "what do you take me for? But it stands to reason that she must be informed of her uncle's death, and that she must order mourning."

"If her uncle has left her money enough to pay for a black gown, she may consider herself lucky," murmured the despondent Rector when he was left alone.

But the prospect was not really so unsatisfactory as that; nor in his heart did he believe that it was. Something would doubtless prove to have been done for Veronica, whose claims had been virtually acknowledged by the late Mr. Trevor, although they had never been urged either by her or by those who from her earliest childhood had given her a home.

It was now a matter of five-and-twenty years since the younger brother of the Rector of Harbury Vale had insisted upon marrying Miss Trevor, notwithstanding his lack of means, while Miss Trevor had insisted on marrying him, despite the opposition of her nearest relatives. There had been no particular harm in Cecil Dimsdale, nor any particular good. A dreamy, inefficient, amiable member of the community, he might have dawdled through life creditably enough for all practical purposes, had he possessed money enough to dawdle upon, and it was not at all improbable that he—or rather his wife—would have been provided with the requisite money if he had not, shortly after his marriage, taken it into his foolish head to do an utterly unpardonable thing. This was not the frittering away of a part of Mrs. Cecil's small fortune in absurd speculations (although the fact that he had done so was subsequently remembered against him), but his abrupt and wholly unexpected secession to the Romish communion. He might, like Moses, have broken all the Ten Commandments at a blow with more hope of ever being forgiven by his stern brother-in-law. His wife, who shared his change of faith, and possibly caused it, was well aware of that; so it must be assumed that her convictions were strong. Be that as it may, she got nothing more from the incensed Samuel, save a solemn and elaborate written anathema, nor did the extreme poverty to which she and her husband were soon reduced avail to soften the heart of that outraged Protestant. What would have become of the luckless pair if they had not gone out in a sailing-boat one day and been capsized and happily drowned, it is impossible to say. Mr. Trevor professed to see

the finger of Providence in the fate which overtook
them ; possibly he was not mistaken.   Their child,
a mere infant at the time, was taken charge of by
the good people at Harbury Vale and brought up
by them as a member of the Church of England ;
but, notwithstanding this latter circumstance, Mr.
Trevor had always declined to see the girl or
recognise her in any way.   She was the child of
wicked parents, he was wont to say, and those who
had chosen to take the responsibility of receiving
her into their family circle must accept the consequences of so rash an act.   For the rest, she had
a little money, inherited from her mother—about
£200 a year, it turned out eventually to be—so that
the Reverend John and his excellent wife did not
consider themselves entitled to any thanks for feed-
ing, clothing and educating her.   Now that she was
of age, she paid for her food and dressed herself
out of the proceeds of her own small fortune.   In
one sense also she had educated herself ; for
Veronica Dimsdale was a young woman of marked
individuality, who formed her opinions and regu-
lated her course of study at first hand—or thought
that she did so.   It was, at all events, neither from
Uncle John nor from Aunt Elizabeth that she had

derived some of the views that she held, and the former was not free from occasional misgivings on her score. The Reverend John did not think it at all desirable that women should know too much, and there were sundry authors whose works he would fain have forbidden his niece to read ; but she had quietly argued the point with him, and, as he had not had the best of the argument, he had yielded with a sigh. His own blameless Lizzie and Martha and Deborah had always submitted cheerfully to the existence of an " Index Expurgatorius " ; but then they were far more docile, and far less eager for information, than Veronica. That may have been one reason why he could not help finding Veronica's society more stimulating than theirs.

CHAPTER II.

VERONICA.

The Harbury Vale Rectory is a low, straggling building, of which the white walls are almost concealed by wistaria, clematis, banksia roses, jasmine and other climbing plants. It stands among green pasture-lands; facing it, and at an almost imperceptibly lower level, flows the broad river, while woods of beech, oak and elm rise gently behind it; so that it is a charmingly pretty place in summer, a frequently flooded place in autumn and winter and an undeniably damp place all the year round. However, it enjoys the advantage of a gravel soil, which may account for the fact that Mr. and Mrs. Dimsdale had successfully reared four children, as well as a niece, during their residence at Harbury Vale, and that their doctor's bill at the end of each year never exceeded a modest total.

Of these four children the two eldest had fulfilled their manifest destiny by espousing curates. Deborah —poor, plain-featured Deborah, for whom no mate had as yet been found—still remained beneath the paternal roof; while Joe, the youngest of the flock, was also for the present at home, and was a walking testimony to the salubrity of his birthplace. Tall, broad-shouldered and well put together, Joe Dimsdale left nothing to be desired in the matter of physique: it was a pity (or, at all events, his mother thought so) that his red hair, his freckled cheeks and irregular features rendered it impossible for anybody to call him good-looking. But Joe himself, who had not yet begun to shave, and who, consequently, seldom examined his countenance in the glass, was very well satisfied with the body in which it had pleased Providence to locate a spirit capable of huge enjoyment. So long as there were hounds to be followed on foot (for the Rectory stables contained but one horse, and to ask that animal to jump over the most insignificant fence would have been much the same thing as asking him to win the Grand National); so long as there were rabbits to be potted and even an occasional partridge to be laid low; so long as Father Thames continued to afford facilities for sculling, canoeing and swimming, the world, in Joe Dimsdale's opinion, was satisfactory enough. Even when there was nothing else to do, there were pretty generally rats to be killed ; and on this March morning Joe, assisted by the man-of-all-work and by his broken-haired fox-terrier, Nipper, was engaged in killing rats, which is a far pleasanter occupation than composing sermons.

It was in the stable-yard that this necessary pro-cess of exterminating vermin was being carried out upon the most approved principles. Joe, with the eager Nipper secured tightly between his legs, was awaiting the moment for each squeaking rat to be released, in turn, by the man-of-all-work from its wire cage. The dog was doing his work admirably, the bodies of the quickly slain lay piled up in the background, and it really seemed a sad pity when only one more victim remained for execution.

" We've come to the last of them, Veronica," said the young fellow regretfully, glancing up at the tall, dark-haired girl who had been a silent spectator of this scientific butchery. " He's a fine big chap though to finish with. Isn't he making a row about it, too !"

Veronica did not reply ; but just at the critical

instant, when the rat was set free, she suddenly
opened her sunshade, which she had been swinging
on one finger, in the dog's face. Away went the
rat; away, after a second of natural bewilderment,
went Nipper in pursuit; and then there was a brief
scene of excitement, terminating—as in that en-
closed space it was pretty certain to terminate—in
a brilliant victory for the attacking forces.

"Now, what in the world made you do that,
Veronica?" asked Joe, in accents which expressed
amused curiosity rather than displeasure.

"Impulse, I suppose," answered the girl. "It
wasn't much use, was it?"

"No, but it might have been; and if it had
you would have grieved me and made Nipper feel
ashamed of himself and let a pestilent animal loose
upon society. You should think of these things
before you act, Veronica; you are far too ready to
yield to your impulses."

The girl laughed a little. She was evidently upon
terms of mutual comprehension with her companion,
and saw that he was only trying to be funny because
he was afraid of having distressed her. "Come
down to the river," she said abruptly; "there are
no rats there."

" Oh ! aren't there, though !" Joe returned.

" Well, I don't so much mind in the case of water-rats ; they have at least a chance for their lives. But the whole thing—everything that goes by the name of sport—is brutal and horrible."

It was impossible for Joe Dimsdale to let such a sweeping assertion as that pass unchallenged. Sincere as his affection and admiration for his cousin were, he felt bound to explain that sport is ennobling, not degrading, and he argued the point with her while they strolled across the grass towards that fence on the bank of the river where they had held many previous colloquies of a more or less desultory character. Veronica and Joe had always been friends, although they differed in temperament almost as much as they did in appearance. Veronica was one of those somewhat rare human beings who, without actual beauty of form or feature, have a personal attractiveness which defies analysis. It may have been her voice, which was low-pitched and had odd breaks in it ; it may have been the clear pallor of her complexion or the natural grace of her movements that distinguished her from the common herd and caused most members of the opposite sex to pay her a homage that she did not covet; but nobody had ever had the hardihood to call her beautiful, much less pretty. She had gray eyes, which grew light or dark in obedience to the stirring of her emotions; she had long, dark eyelashes, and, colourless though her face was, she conveyed the impression of being in perfect health. When you had said that you had said all that could be said for her in a physical sense; for her mouth was too large, her nose was of no particular shape, and the outline of her person was rather angular. Her conversation, to be sure, was interesting, because she was in the habit of saying what she thought, and her thoughts were usually original. She read a great deal; she was considered clever; Mr. Mostyn, the great poet, critic and philosopher, had not hesitated to predict that she had a literary future before her.

The same eminent authority had not felt able to use equally hopeful language with respect to Joe, whose future for the moment had become an unknown quantity, owing to his repeated failures to pass the requisite examinations for admission into the Army. Yet Joe, too, was clever in some ways, being singularly observant and often shrewd in his judgments of men and things. "But what," his father would pertinently ask, " is the use of qualities which cannot be turned to any practical account? What is the use of knowing the note of every bird that flies and being acquainted with the whereabouts of every fox's earth within twenty miles and being able to prattle off the pedigree of any hound in England at a moment's notice? To have acquired such information implies great diligence and a carefully cultivated memory; yet when you lay an examination-paper before the fellow and put a simple question to him about a subject which he has been studying for months, he'll declare that he has forgotten all about it."

It was natural enough that Mr. Dimsdale should think his son very unsatisfactory, and scarcely surprising that the neighbourhood at large should find itself in sympathetic agreement with Mr. Dimsdale; but Veronica was always ready to take up the cudgels on Joe's behalf. There was scarcely a subject upon which these two thought alike; the one was prone to be poetical and visionary, the other, despite his inability to adapt himself to the conditions of his lot, was eminently practical; they had not the same friends, nor did they follow the same pursuits. Nevertheless, they understood one

another, and they were under the not altogether
erroneous impression that nobody else understood
either of them. Thus, although they were constantly
disputing, they never quarrelled ; and the discussion
upon which they were now engaged was conducted
in an entirely amicable spirit.

" That is all very well, Joseph," remarked Veronica,
resting her elbows upon the railing and swinging
her sunshade to and fro above the turbid water,
" but you will never persuade me that killing is not
cruel. You would think it atrociously cruel if a
race of creatures much bigger and better armed
than yourself were to amuse themselves by hunting
you to death."

" Never said it wasn't cruel, my dear," returned
Joe, who had seated himself sideways upon the
fence and had lighted a short black pipe ; " I only
said it was necessary. Do you suppose sheep and
oxen like being slaughtered for your dinner ?"

" Well, you know, I did try being a vegetarian for
several months, and I only gave it up because Uncle
John's arguments about manure seemed to be un-
answerable. I grant you that the whole scheme of
Nature is cruel and that we are bound to prey upon
one another ; but there is all the difference in the

world between slaying to support life and slaying for the mere pleasure of shedding blood."

"Veronica," said Joe, removing his pipe from his lips and pointing it at her didactically, "I will tell you something which, being a woman, you can't know. Man is by nature a bloodthirsty animal, and unless you provide him with some legitimate outlet for his instincts, the odds are that he will play Old Harry with himself and everybody else. Of course, when I say man, I mean *men*, not abnormal beings, like your friend Mr. Mostyn and a few others, who can get along quite comfortably upon tea and toast and talk——"

"Mr. Mostyn is one of the greatest men of this century," interjected Veronica calmly.

"Very well; he is all that, if you like, and perhaps it isn't his fault that he was born a muff. But you'll allow that he is abnormal. Goodness only knows what sort of a ruffian the ordinary, everyday Englishman, such as your humble servant, would develop into if he were forbidden to kill birds and beasts and fishes in a skilful and sportsmanlike style."

"I can't quite see how you reconcile those sentiments with your love of animals," Veronica remarked.

" I don't," answered Joe with a grin ; " I leave them to reconcile themselves as best they can, like predestination and free-will and a heap of other contraries which manage to run in double harness somehow or other. All that I can tell you is that I do love animals and I do like shooting and fishing, when I can get the chance. I ain't a murderer, but if only I could have passed those blessed exams., I expect I should have liked fighting too."

Veronica made no immediate rejoinder, but continued to gaze down reflectively at the river. Her cousin's last words had given another turn to her thoughts, and she did not deem it necessary to explain to what she was alluding when, after a time, she remarked, " It's a dreadful pity !"

" Yes, it's a pity," the young fellow agreed, " but there's no good in crying about it. I did my best— though nobody but you will ever believe I did—and I was beaten. It wouldn't make other people happier to be told how disappointed I am. In fact, I suspect I should deprive them of their only solace if I forced them to sympathise with me instead of groaning over me."

Veronica laughed. She had a loud, abrupt, but not unmelodious laugh, which she never attempted to repress, and which sometimes escaped her at inappropriate moments. " Perhaps you would," she said. " And what will you do now ?"

" Well, I was thinking of a land agency. I believe it's what I'm best fitted for. Either that or emigration."

" Oh, I can't let you emigrate !" Veronica hastily exclaimed. " What should I do without you ?"

" The great and good Mostyn would remain in England for your comfort and consolation."

" Joseph, there are times when you disgust me ! Oh, dear ! I wish Uncle Trevor would die and leave me all his estates. Then I would make you my agent at once."

It was at this dramatically opportune juncture that Mrs. Dimsdale, with a knitted shawl flung over her shoulders, the *Times* in her hand and a voice attuned to the melancholy circumstances, stepped out from the adjacent shrubbery to say : " Veronica dear, I have been looking for you everywhere. I am sorry to tell you that your poor uncle is gone. Here is the announcement of his death. I dare say you would like to see what they say about him."

Joe produced a very large silk pocket-handkerchief and held it before his eyes, sobbing aloud.

"Oh!" he moaned; "this is hard to bear! So righteous, so benevolent, so fondly affectionate to his nearest relatives! And then to be cut off, without the least warning, at the comparatively early age of eighty-something! I do think, mother, that you might have broken the sad intelligence more gently. And please, m'm, does the paper say anything about deceased's will?"

"Don't be indecent, Joe," remonstrated Mrs. Dimsdale, smothering a laugh. "He really was a good man, according to his lights—at any rate, many people thought so—and he was a connection of ours by marriage, you know. No; of course there is nothing about the will yet."

Veronica, who had been glancing at the obituary panegyric of which a portion has already been quoted, handed the newspaper back to her aunt and remarked: "I can tell you how he has disposed of his property; Mr. Horace Trevor inherits everything."

"Not quite *everything*, dear," corrected Mrs. Dimsdale. "There are sure to be charitable bequests; and your aunt Julia, I believe, obtained a promise from her brother that you should receive a substantial legacy."

" Did she ?" asked Veronica indifferently. " I don't think I want it. I have quite as much money as I need."

" In that case, my dear," observed Joe, " you probably stand alone amidst the greedy inhabitants of an over-populated world. But I have always maintained that you are unique. As for me, who am no better than I should be, I trust you will excuse my reminding you of what you were saying just now, and if you should find that you have come in for a trifle of twenty or thirty thousand pounds which you don't need, nothing will give me greater satisfaction than to relieve you of the burden."

But even Mrs. Dimsdale's sanguine anticipations did not rise above the half, or more probably the quarter of such a sum, and in truth there was little reason to expect that Mr. Trevor, the most obstinate and unforgiving of men, would prove to have recognised posthumous obligations towards one with whom, during his lifetime, he had steadily refused to have anything to do. Mrs. Dimsdale wrote a letter of quasi-condolence to Mrs. Mansfield, the only surviving sister of the deceased philanthropist, but received no reply, and after a few days hope died away within her breast. It was disappointing, but it was of a piece with that horrid old man's conduct (he was a horrid old man again now) from first to last. "And, after all," concluded Mrs. Dimsdale, in her optimistic way, "Veronica is certain to marry well, which will answer all the purpose. Perhaps, if she had come into a little fortune all to herself now, she would only have done something dreadfully foolish with it before she could have been stopped."

Then, one morning, a letter, addressed in a clerkly hand, was delivered to Veronica, which she opened and perused with feelings of stupefaction rather than of exultation—

"*Lincoln's Inn Fields, W.C., March* 18, 189—.

"*Madam,—We are instructed by the executors of the late Mr. Samuel Trevor to inform you that, under his will, you succeed to his estate of Broxham Hall, in the county of Norfolk, together with personalty, of which the exact amount cannot at present be ascertained, but which, we may say, will probably exceed one hundred thousand pounds (£100,000). As you will, no doubt, wish to be placed in possession of further particulars, and as it is desirable that we should have a personal interview with you, may we beg that you will favour us with a call at*

*an early date ? Or, should you prefer it, our Mr. Walton
will wait upon you at your present residence.—We are,
Madam, your obedient servants,*

"WALTON, JOHNSON, HOPKINS *and* CO.,

"*Solicitors.*"

Veronica read the above letter through several
times, with increasing bewilderment. Then she
handed it over to the Rector, who had noticed
the superscription and had been surveying her in-
quiringly over his spectacles.

"Uncle John," she said, "will you look at this,
please, and tell me whether it is genuine or not ?
I hope it is only a stupid practical joke."

Mr. Dimsdale was a good deal amused at the
time by what struck him as being the oddest com-
ment he had ever heard in his life upon a piece of
extraordinary good luck; yet subsequent events led
him more than once to doubt whether the late Mr.
Trevor had not in truth meant to perpetrate a grim
jest at the expense of sundry survivors by bequeathing
money and lands to an utterly inexperienced girl.

CHAPTER III.

THE PREACHER AND THE POET.

THE following day was a Sunday, and letters are not delivered on Sundays at Harbury Vale; still, those who are in a hurry for their correspondence may obtain it by applying at the village post-office, so that the Rectory folks usually halted there on their way to church. This practice, as a rule, possessed little interest for Veronica, who seldom received a letter on any day of the week; but now she was, for once, rather anxious to hear whether there was anything for her, because she thought it not improbable that her aunt, Mrs. Mansfield, might have written. And her anticipations were verified. A thick, black-edged envelope was handed to her, a similar one was awarded to Mrs. Dimsdale, and as the party resumed its march, to the accompaniment of a noisy peal of bells, each lady perused her missive, Veronica silently, Mrs. Dimsdale with interjectional grunts and subdued expressions of approval.

Mrs. Mansfield's letter to her niece was, as the latter had expected it to be, an invitation. " Mr. Walton tells me that he must see you," this good-natured lady, who had never shared her late brother's peculiar prejudices, wrote, " and of course I shall be only too glad to give you house-room and to do anything that I can for you. Your position altogether is so extraordinary and so unforeseen that one hardly realises it yet or sees what steps you ought to take ; but I should think your best plan will be to stay with me until things have unravelled themselves a little and some sort of scheme can be formed for your future life. I ought to have answered Mrs. Dimsdale's letter before this : my only excuse is that I have been literally *stunned* and unable to write to anybody. As I think I told you, it was quite an understood thing that poor Horace was to succeed to the property, and although there had been a coolness of late between him and your uncle, I never for one moment imagined that Samuel would go to the extreme length of altering his will ! I cannot help thinking that he must have done it in a moment of mental aberration, and that he would have repaired such an act of injustice if he had lived a little longer. Not that there is the slightest intention of disputing the will or that I at all grudge you your wonderful good luck—pray don't suppose that, my dear! Still, it *is* hard upon Horace, who, if he isn't exactly a saint or a Methodist minister, has always been quite as well-behaved as other young men. However, I will tell you all about it when you come. Meanwhile, I am always your affectionate aunt, JULIA MANSFIELD."

"Well, that disposes of one difficulty," Mrs. Dimsdale remarked, in a tone of satisfaction, as she stuffed her letter into her pocket and passed her arm through her niece's. "Very kind and thoughtful of your Aunt Julia, I'm sure, and she writes in the nicest possible way about you. What a mercy it is that you *have* an Aunt Julia to go to!"

"I have an Aunt Elizabeth who has satisfied my modest requirements pretty well so far," remarked Veronica, smiling.

"Ah, so far! but everything is changed now. I am only a poor old country mouse, and I shouldn't have known in the least how to be of service to you under these altered circumstances; whereas Mrs. Mansfield is a woman of the world, who will be able to tell you exactly what you ought to do. Who is this young Horace, who seems to have been dis-inherited in your favour? Not a nephew of old Mr. Trevor's, surely? I never heard of his having had a brother."

"Only a distant kinsman whom he adopted, I believe," answered Veronica, "but I really never thought of asking any questions upon the subject." She walked on for some yards, paying no heed to Mrs. Dimsdale's continuous prattle. Then she ex-claimed suddenly: "How odd you are, Aunt Elizabeth! Why should you be so delighted at my having come into all this money? You do not profit by it—not necessarily, at least."

"That remains to be seen," struck in Deborah before her mother could reply. "From what I know of you, Veronica, I should say that the very first use to which you would put your money would be to give some of it away to your friends."

Deborah was a thick-set, red-haired little person, much given to good works, greatly beloved by the poor of the parish and notorious in her family for the innocent indiscretion of her utterances. She was upon the point of adding something about its being more blessed to give than to receive when she

herself received a doubtful blessing in the shape of a
pinch in the fleshy part of the arm from her brother,
which caused her to break into a short, sharp
squeal.

"Shut up, Deb!" growled Joe under his breath;
and Deborah shut up with her accustomed docility,
though she was unable to see what she had done to
earn this discourteous command.

Mrs. Dimsdale, who was in truth a most unselfish
woman, was answering that she rejoiced in her
niece's good fortune just as she would have rejoiced
in the good fortune of one of her daughters. "And
besides," she added cheerfully, "we shall all come
and stay with you at Broxham sometimes, if you
will have us; and there will be the shooting for Joe,
you know, and——"

"Oh, that!" interrupted Veronica, with a quick
wave of her hand. "But, Aunt Elizabeth, aren't
you at all sorry?—not the least little bit?"

"Sorry, my dear!" ejaculated the good lady;
"what *do* you mean? Now don't, please don't, say
that you are! That would be too perverse of you,
and it would worry me all through the service, so
that I shouldn't be able to fix my mind upon my
prayers."

Veronica, therefore, held her peace, and they all went into church.

The Rector preached a very fine sermon that morning. It was not the one to which allusion has already been made, and which had been delivered on the previous Sunday; but it dealt with a kindred subject, and he had chosen for his text " How hardly shall they that have riches enter into the kingdom of Heaven." Veronica, as she always did, listened attentively to her uncle's discourse, every word of which seemed to apply so exactly to her own case that she was inclined every now and then to think he might have dealt a little more mercifully with her. He began by confessing frankly, on behalf of himself and humanity at large, that riches are what we all desire. As a matter of theory, we may be willing to admit that there are other good things— health, for example—which rank infinitely higher; but as a matter of practice, at least nine-tenths of us devote our brains, our energies and the best part of our lives to the acquisition of wealth. When we acquire it, if we ever do acquire it, we probably find that it has not been worth all that trouble. But the Rector said that he did not, for the moment, wish to dwell upon that aspect of the question; what he wished to emphasise was the enormous power of money and the consequent responsibility attaching to those who possessed it. To say that wealth rules the world was, he declared, a mere truism, and he proceeded to show how the peace of Europe was now in the keeping, not of Emperors, Kings, Chancellors of Parliaments, but of certain eminent financiers whom he did not name and of whom the majority of his hearers had most likely never heard. And what was true of the world was true, he urged, of all communities, large and small. Whether we liked to acknowledge it or not, the fact remained that we all respected a rich man—respected him not for any talent or perseverance that he might have displayed in enriching himself, but simply and solely because he was rich, because he had houses, lands, horses, flowers and other luxuries which belong only to the few. We allowed him to dictate to us upon social matters; we were gratified when he condescended to seek our friendship; we recognised him, in short, as our superior. "And so, in actual truth, he is," added the preacher. "He can accomplish what it would be vain for us even to attempt; his power, for good or evil, is as much greater and wider than ours as the power of his

Creator is greater and wider than his own; isolated by reason of a power of which it is impossible for him to divest himself, he learns—or fails to learn—the secret of that sadness which has ever been discernible upon the countenances of 'those who bear rule and are obeyed.'"

Then, of course, it was easy to point out how the rich man, between the horns of a dilemma, was a less enviable being than he might appear at first sight. Either he realised his position, realising at the same time that he must not look for much happiness in this world, or he did not realise it—in which case his prospects for the next could hardly be contemplated without a shudder. Mr. Dimsdale had eloquence and a vibrating, sympathetic voice; he always conveyed the impression of being very much in earnest; when he had worked himself up to the requisite pitch of emotion, his subject commonly swept him off his legs, and the ideals he was wont to set up at such times were, perhaps, a shade too lofty for human attainment. At any rate, by the time that he had made an end of explaining what a rich man's duties were, and how exceedingly unlikely any rich man was to fulfil them, one at least of his audience was disposed to add a fresh petition

to the Litany—" From battle, murder and sudden
death, and from a sudden accession of fortune, good
Lord, deliver us !"

But the fresh air and the sunshine outside, together
with the somewhat irreverent comments of the
Rector's only son, were not without a bracing effect
upon Veronica's flagging spirits.

" I regard that sermon as a gross outrage upon
good taste," Joe declared. " If he had told you in
so many words that it was your bounden duty to
restore the chancel and put a new roof on the church,
he couldn't have expressed his meaning more plainly.
I am quite ashamed of him, and, in the unavoidable
absence of the reverend gentleman, I beg to offer
you a full apology. Personally, I may say that,
while we congratulate you upon having succeeded to
a pot of money, and are convinced that you will
make a wise use of it, we wish to goodness it hadn't
been quite such a large pot. Because, you see, we
don't want to lose you."

" Thank you, Joseph !" exclaimed Veronica gratefully ; " you always know how to say the right
thing."

" I can when I like," answered Joe, with quiet
complacency.

"And you really will miss me a little? Aunt Elizabeth doesn't seem to think that my departure will cause any perceptible blank in the household."

"You know very well that you will be missed," said Joe. "I wouldn't be morbid if I were you. Take example by me. Ain't I bearing up like a man, in spite of everything? Not that I am going to stay on here without you. No, thanks! I shall be off to Australia or the Cape or the Western States of America as soon as possible."

"You forget that you are going to be my land-agent," observed Veronica, smiling.

"I am not sure that you will want one, my dear; and if you did, I should be hardly ready to accept the situation for a year or two. But let's make the best of things. We shall meet again some day, when we are old and uninteresting, and 'when the glow of early thought has declined in feeling's dull decay.' That isn't the sort of poetry that you admire though—and, by Jove! here comes the sort of poet whom you do admire. Farewell for the present—I'm off! There isn't room for me and him in one small meadow."

If Veronica admired the tall, spare, elderly gentle-man who was sauntering towards her along the river

bank, and who removed his wideawake hat, disclosing
a fine crop of curly grizzled hair, on her approach,
she was by no means alone in so doing. Cyril
Mostyn's niche in the Temple of Fame had been
won many years before by the refined and scholarly
verses which he continued to publish at rare in-
tervals; as a critic he was perhaps even better
known than as a poet, while his social pre-eminence
was all the more an established fact because he had
never taken the slightest trouble to earn or retain
it.   At the age of fifty, or thereabouts, he was still a
singularly handsome man ; he knew everybody worth
knowing, literary, scientific, political and fashionable,
and when he occupied his comfortable bachelor
quarters in London, he dined out every night of his
life.   Latterly, however, he had taken to spending a
great deal of his time at the rustic cottage on the
banks of the Thames which he had purchased chiefly
with a view to escaping the importunities of his
friends.

"Have you been to church?" he inquired, in the
low, mellow accents which were counted among his
personal attractions.

Mr. Mostyn himself was *parcus cultor et infrequens*
of established rites, having indeed written some

rather cruel and incisive essays upon the subject of revealed religion; still, he was to be seen every now and then in places of worship, and he had never publicly abjured Christianity.

"Yes," answered Veronica, "I have been to church; but I don't think I feel much the better for it. Uncle John has made me wretched by preaching a perfectly beautiful sermon to prove the impossibility of forcing a camel through the eye of a needle. And the worst of it is that, all of a sudden and through no fault of my own, I have become a camel!"

"So I hear," Mr. Mostyn observed, smiling and gazing at her. "I should have congratulated you, only I felt quite sure that you would not want to be congratulated. Poor old Trevor! . . . and, still more, poor young Trevor! . . . and, most of all, perhaps, poor you!"

"Oh, it is horrid!" exclaimed Veronica disconsolately. "What *could* have made him do it!"

Mr. Mostyn shrugged his shoulders. "Lack of self-control, I suppose," he answered. "The young man is not a religious young man, and it was discovered, I believe, that he had been backing horses. Then there was a scene, and a will was made which would probably have been destroyed if there had been time. Authors are not the only people who sometimes put pen to paper unadvisedly."

" The more I think of it all," sighed Veronica, "the more plainly I see that a dreadful injustice has been done, of which I have no business to take advantage."

" But there is no imaginable way in which you can avoid taking advantage of it."

Veronica laughed. " Oh, yes," she returned; " it is as simple as one of the hard cases in *Vanity Fair.* ' A, a rustic maiden, inherits a large fortune from an aged relative whom she has never seen, and who has always treated B as his heir. B, a well-conducted young man, temporarily estranged from the old gentleman by some trifling difference, would doubtless have been reinstated, had the latter lived a few months longer. A is neither fitted for her new position nor anxious to occupy it. What is A to do ? Answer received, adjudged correct—Marry B.' "

" Well," said Mr. Mostyn, smiling, " that would solve a difficulty, no doubt. It only remains to obtain B's assent to the arrangement."

" And B is an unknown quantity."

" Not to me ; I have met him several times in London. He is a nice-looking, nice-mannered young gentleman of the approved pattern, and would be quite willing to do anything that he was told, I should think, provided that it was not too unpleasant ; and it is obviously superfluous to add——" Here Mr. Mostyn spread out his hands and made a little bow. " At the same time," he resumed, " nothing can be more certain than that, after you had lived with Mr. Horace Trevor for a few months, you would be arranging the terms of an amicable separation. Your husband, my dear Miss Dimsdale, will have to be a literary man ; that happens, fortunately or unfortunately, to be indispensable, and I should be very much surprised to hear that young Trevor had opened a single book, except a sporting novel or a ' Ruff's Guide,' since he left Oxford."

" What is to be done, then ?" asked Veronica.

She was in the habit of asking Mr. Mostyn what was to be done whenever she stood in need of counsel ; for she had the highest opinion of his wisdom and she had been the recipient of many tokens of his goodwill. The advice that he gave her now, in answer to a more detailed statement of her perplexities than she had as yet vouchsafed to anybody, was certainly sound, so far as it went. He urged her to do nothing in a hurry; he reminded her that responsibility cannot be thrown off, like an extra blanket, simply because it is more comfortable to get rid of it; and for immediate and practical questions he referred her to the lawyers.

"One does not want to be bothered about money," he concluded; "it is a nuisance to have too little of it and a nuisance to have too much. You must expect to be a good deal bothered for the next few months; but after that, I hope, you will be able to turn your attention to more important things again. Have you been stringing any more rhymes together?"

"Yes," answered Veronica, laughing and colouring slightly; "but I am not going to show them to you. You only praise my rubbish because you wish to be kind and encouraging."

"No," Mr. Mostyn assured her gravely, "I don't do that. I never tell polite fibs upon the subject of art, which I take to be the one serious thing in this world of irony and farce and charlatanism. All that I have said to you is that your work shows great promise. Whether the promise will be fulfilled or not depends upon a variety of considerations—your sex and this necessary change in your social surroundings being, to my mind, very much against you. However, we shall see. One thing that I may be able to do for you now is to introduce you to men and women whose chief interest in life is literature. Rubbing up against them will do you good, even if you find them rather disappointing from a conversational point of view."

" Oh, thank you !" exclaimed Veronica gratefully. " I must go now, or I shall be late for dinner. I suppose rich people don't have to dine early on Sundays, do they ? At any rate, I know Aunt Julia doesn't, and I know she is always at home on Sunday afternoons. If you should be in London on a Sunday some time, perhaps you would look in upon us."

The great man graciously promised to do so. It was pretty well understood among Mr. Mostyn's fashionable friends that he did not expect to be invited to anything except dinners, and that his presence even at a dinner-party was a favour which demanded suitable acknowledgment; but Veronica Dimsdale was privileged. He had a sort of paternal affection for her, and allowed her to take liberties which children may take with their parents, literary and other

CHAPTER IV.

VERONICA MAKES INQUIRIES.

THE Honourable Mrs. Mansfield was a well-preserved widow of between fifty and sixty, with whom life had gone as smoothly as she had permitted it to go. Absolute, unbroken smoothness is, no doubt, repellent to human nature, as being far too monotonous and affording none of those contrasts which enable us to determine whether we are contented or the reverse at any given moment; so this fortunate lady, who had neither husband, nor children, nor monetary worries, nor bad health to distress her, had felt bound during many years to seek out grounds of dissatisfaction for herself, though she had been sometimes hard put to it to discover them. Her brother Samuel, to do him justice, had always been ready to oblige any fellow-creature who might be suffering from lack of causeless annoyance, and there had been frequent differences, attaining almost to the dignity of quarrels, between him and Mrs. Mansfield; but now poor Samuel had departed for scenes where bickering is presumably unknown, and notwithstanding the comfortable little legacy of five thousand pounds which he had bequeathed to his "beloved sister Julia," the latter would have been inconsolable had he not displayed the most considerate inconsideration by disposing of the bulk of his property after a fashion which was enough to make any sensible woman wring her hands in despair. It really was rather hard, at her time of life, to be saddled with the care of a girl who was decidedly odd, probably wilful and quite obviously unfitted to stand alone. One must not shirk such duties, distasteful though they may be. One cannot turn one's back upon one's poor sister's child. One must look forward, with such courage as can be mustered, to endless troubles and vexations. One must expect no thanks, and perhaps very little success; one must endeavour not to think evil of the dead, and to assume charitably that Samuel, when he did a perfectly idiotic thing, was not altogether responsible for his actions. This was what Mrs. Mansfield was saying to herself as she sat before the fire in her pretty drawing-room in South Audley Street awaiting the advent of the niece whom she had summoned. She knew that Veronica was odd, because she had already had the girl to stay with her once—on that occasion when her well-meant attempt to effect a reconciliation between the uncle and niece had fallen through. She anticipated trouble, because—since it was evident that the heiress could not dispense with a chaperon—the finger of fate seemed to point unmistakably towards the person upon whom that function must devolve. And she was dreadfully distressed because poor Horace Trevor, whom she had always liked and tried to befriend, was left out in the cold, without, in reality, having done anything at all to deserve such treatment.

All this did not prevent her from warmly embracing the tall, sable-clad girl who was shown into the room just as it was becoming dark enough to ring for lamps.

"My dear child!" she exclaimed, "I am so delighted to have you with me again! Come and sit down and have some tea; you must be perished with cold after your railway journey in this bitter wind!"

Veronica surveyed the pretty old lady, whose hair was drawn up high above her forehead, whose diamonds flashed in the firelight and whose slim fingers continued to clasp her own after they had both seated themselves. She had not yet quite made up her mind whether she liked Mrs. Mansfield or not. Certainly, Aunt Julia had been kind, and had written her affectionate letters from time to time; but her kindness had not been of the practical order displayed by the good people of Harbury Vale, nor was there any reason to suppose that the new order of things was welcome to a lady who had always seemed to acquiesce philosophically enough in the sentence of banishment pronounced upon the child of erring parents.

" Aren't you disgusted ?" she asked presently.

" Oh, not with *you*, dear !" Mrs. Mansfield replied, laughing a little. " Of course, I do think it is rather a pity—as much for your sake as for anybody's."

" So do I, I am sure !" agreed Veronica. " Still, we may perhaps hit upon some means of putting matters a little more straight than they are at present. I want you to tell me all about Mr. Horace Trevor ; you said in your letter that you would."

Mrs. Mansfield declined to do that upon the spur

of the moment. She declared that neither she nor the injured Horace nor anybody else had ever dreamed of attaching the smallest blame to a palpably innocent supplanter, and that, upon the whole, it was a case of least said soonest mended. But later in the evening she was induced to become more communicative. Sitting in the drawing-room with her niece, after a little dinner which had been admirably cooked and served, and in the course of which she had felt moved towards a certain sympathy of intercourse, she narrated the story of the difference that had proved so terribly expensive to the late Mr. Trevor's reputed heir.

" It really was too ridiculous !—the sort of thing that nobody in the world except Samuel would ever have wasted a second thought upon. As if all young men didn't bet occasionally ! But you know what he was ; or rather, perhaps, you don't know. Next to Roman Catholics, I believe, he looked upon gamblers and what he used to call ' Sabbath-breakers ' as being about the most hopelessly wicked beings on earth ; so when it transpired that Horace had been to the Grand Prix last year, and had, unfortunately, backed the horse that didn't win into the bargain, there was a fine fuss. Of course, there had been rows before, and for my own part I didn't expect that this one would have more serious consequences than the others, although, now that one comes to look back, it certainly did lead to a rather more prolonged estrangement. You see, Samuel, when he was put out, had a way of saying the most grossly insulting things in Christian phraseology; and Horace, good-tempered as he is, was sometimes provoked to retaliate. He tells me he did use the expression ' damned hypocrisy,' which he ought not to have done; still, I am bound to confess that I myself have more than once accused my brother of the same thing—minus the adjective."

Veronica broke into one of her abrupt fits of laughter, in which Mrs. Mansfield, after a moment of hesitation, joined.

" Not that it is any laughing matter for poor Horace," the latter observed ruefully.

" What is he like ?" Veronica asked.

" Well, he is a nice, clean-looking little fellow, with short brown hair and gray eyes and no moustache ; there are dozens and dozens of them about. It seems to me that men weren't turned out so exactly after the same pattern when I was young; but perhaps that is a fallacy."

" I didn't mean in appearance," said Veronica.

" Oh, as far as character goes, I think he might be placed very near the top of his class; though I don't say that that is the very highest class of all. Personally, I have no particular love for immaculate youths; I like them to be just a bit naughty, so long as they are gentlemen; don't you ?"

" I like them to be gentlemen," answered Veronica, "and I like them to be of some use in the world—or, at least, to try."

" Well, my dear," returned Mrs. Mansfield, a little sharply, " Horace would have been of great use in the world if he had been allowed to become a country gentleman—which is what Nature intended him to be. So far, he really hasn't had a chance. Samuel forced him to resign his commission in the 23rd Hussars because he said that cavalry officers were a godless crew; then he kept him for several years kicking his heels about in London without any occupation; and now, at last, he cuts him off with a miserable legacy of ten thousand pounds, which, he says in his will, is equivalent to an allowance of five hundred pounds a year; though everybody knows that four per cent. is the very outside that can be obtained upon reasonable security."

"What *could* have made him put me in Mr. Horace Trevor's place?" ejaculated Veronica meditatively. "Did he by any chance think that Nature had intended me to be a country gentleman?"

"My dear, I can't tell you what he thought. He may have had some qualms of conscience about the way in which he treated your poor mother, or he may have nominated you simply because he was in a rage and because he couldn't think of anybody else. Most likely he knew that if he left Broxham to me I should immediately hand the place over to Horace. But really, when one begins attempting to account for the actions of such a man as Samuel was, the imagination reels!"

Veronica nodded, and asked no more questions that evening. At breakfast the next day, however, she stated quietly that she was going to Lincoln's-Inn Fields to see Mr. Walton, as she had not quite made up her mind what to do about her inheritance.

"I don't know that there is very much to be done about it, except to take possession of it when it is handed over by the executors," Mrs. Mansfield said; "and Mr. Walton will call here, if you write him a line. It would be more to the purpose to decide how and where you are to live in future."

"But that will have to depend a good deal upon what Mr. Walton says. I think I had better go to his office; I shall be more sure of securing his undivided attention there."

"When I was young," observed Mrs. Mansfield— "I am sorry to keep on using that phrase, but it is perpetually being forced upon me—it would have been considered most improper for a girl of your age to go off into the City all alone."

"But it isn't considered improper now."

"No, it isn't considered improper now. In some ways you are curiously modern, Veronica; I noticed that when you were here before, and I can't think how you arrived at modernity, living down in the depths of the country. Something in the general atmosphere of the age, I suppose. Well, if you never do anything worse than hunt up a musty old lawyer in his lair, I shall not feel entitled to remonstrate with you."

So presently Veronica was borne in a swift hansom to Lincoln's Inn Fields, where she was received by a tall, elderly gentleman, who at once set to work to explain the various provisions of his late client's testament.

"I am sure you have made it all most beautifully

clear," Veronica said, after several fruitless attempts
to check the flow of his discourse, "but what I more
particularly wanted to ask you was whether you
know my uncle's real motive for disinheriting Mr.
Horace Trevor."

"Well," replied the lawyer, smiling; "I believe
that he did not approve of young Mr. Trevor's
habits."

"But are young Mr. Trevor's habits so very
objectionable? I have heard nothing against him
so far, except that he sometimes bets and that he
once went to the races on a Sunday."

"As far as I am aware, you could not have heard
much more than that against him. I have known
Horace Trevor from his boyhood, and I should say
that very few young men in his position could show
so clean a record."

"Then you agree with me that he has been
abominably ill-treated?"

"I would rather not express any opinion as to
that, Miss Dimsdale. I think he has been exceedingly foolish, and I have often told him so. Knowing what Mr. Trevor's religious views were, he ought
to have had the common-sense to abstain from
running counter to them; and he has nobody but

himself to blame for what has happened. I say
nothing about the payment of his debts; the amount
was trifling on each occasion, and we all know that
young men with expectations are apt to be thoughtless and extravagant. But why the deuce—why in
the world, I mean—he must needs attend a race-
meeting on a Sunday, when every other day of the
week was open to him, passes my poor powers of
comprehension !"

"Oh, I like him all the better for that," Veronica
declared. "If he didn't think he was committing
any sin by spending Sunday in that way, he was
quite right to have the courage of his opinions. I
only wanted to find out whether there was the
slightest excuse for his having been deprived of his
inheritance. As it is, I shall probably restore it to
him. I suppose that can be done quite legally?"

"Oh, yes; you can legally dispose of your property in any way that you may think fit," answered
Mr. Walton, looking rather amused.

"Then perhaps you will kindly undertake the
business for me when the time comes. I cannot
give you positive instructions just yet, because I
don't think I ought to act in a hurry, and, in any
case, I think I should be justified in keeping part of

the money for myself. I believe my uncle meant to leave me something, and I have quite decided to retain a certain amount — ten thousand pounds would be enough, I should think—in order that I may help out a young cousin of mine who has failed for the Army, and whom we propose to send now to a gentleman farmer to study agriculture, so that he may be qualified for a land-agency some day. That, of course, will entail expense; and I have other claims upon me besides."

"I see," answered the lawyer gravely. "Ten thousand pounds is a good deal of money; still, you might, under all the circumstances, assume that your uncle intended to bequeath as much to you. Your purpose, then, as I understand, is to hand over the residue of the personalty and the whole of the real property to Horace Trevor?"

"I believe that is what I ought to do; but, as I tell you, I cannot speak quite positively to-day."

"I hope," said Mr. Walton, "you will excuse me for remarking that you are the most extraordinarily unselfish person I have ever met during a tolerably long experience of my fellow men and women."

"I can quite understand your thinking so," answered Veronica; "but the truth is that I have no wish at all to be rich. It might be my duty to give up the property to Mr. Horace Trevor even if I wanted to retain it; but, as a matter of fact, I don't. It would be far more of a burden than a satisfaction to me."

"Such as it is, my dear young lady, I am afraid you will have to make the best of it," the lawyer returned, with a short laugh. "The wishes of the testator can hardly be set aside with propriety simply because they do not happen to accord with your own. Moreover, there is another small obstacle which you seem to have overlooked: you have still to reckon with Horace Trevor."

"You think perhaps that he would not accept the property as a gift from me?"

"I don't think about the matter; I am perfectly sure that he would not. And I may add that no gentleman would or could do so."

"I don't see that at all," said Veronica. "It is a simple question of putting wrong right, and he must know that it is. As for the testator's wishes, it is absurd to imagine that he ever meant that will to stand. By tearing it up I am only doing what he would have done if he had lived a little longer."

"Unfortunately, there is no method of ascertaining that. Meanwhile, the property is not yours to deal with; so that you will have time for reflection."

He rose as he spoke—meaning, perhaps, to convey a hint that his time was of value—and held out his hand. "I am sure, Miss Dimsdale," he said, smiling, "that a little reflection will convince you of the impossibility of carrying out your present idea. You will have to hit upon some more feasible scheme for impoverishing yourself."

Veronica went away with an uneasy impression that she had made a fool of herself and had seemed anxious to earn a character for unselfishness upon very easy and inexpensive terms. Nevertheless, the lawyer had not convinced her. She still felt that she must not profit by an accident and that Horace Trevor must, somehow or other, be reinstated in his rightful position. The only question was how this was to be contrived, in the face of conventional prejudices the cogency of which could not but be acknowledged.

CHAPTER V.

THE INJURED INNOCENT.

VERONICA returned to South Audley Street in time for luncheon, and found a smart, military-looking old gentleman in a tightly buttoned frock-coat seated with her aunt. This was Mrs. Mansfield's brother-in-law, Lord Chippenham, who had succeeded to the family title and estates somewhat late in life, after rising to the rank of Lieutenant-General and achieving a sufficiency of renown in sundry of those small wars which afford opportunity to the modern British soldier. He was now sixty-five years of age and looked a good ten years younger, being blessed with a fine constitution, a cheerful temper and a set of features which had once upon a time worked havoc with the hearts of susceptible ladies. Even in his gray old age he continued to be very fond of the society of the opposite sex, preferring the young and pretty ones to those whose faces showed signs of wear and tear, but displaying the most amiable politeness to all. He shook hands with Veronica, and began calling her " my dear " at once.

" I am one of your poor uncle's executors, you know," he announced, " and I hear you have just been seeing the other. I was upon the point of saying I wished I was one of your trustees, but that would have been hardly true, for it's no joke, upon my word, to be a trustee ! In my opinion, trustees ought to have been appointed, all the same. Well, well ! let us hope that it will be all right. And how did you get on with old Walton ? Found him rather a formal, cut-and-dry old chap, I dare say."

" No; I don't think I noticed that he was that," answered Veronica, upon whom Mr. Walton's personality had not produced a very strong impression one way or the other. " But he snubbed me a good deal."

" You don't say so ! Well, my dear, I'll promise not to snub you, though I'm afraid I shall have to refer you to Mr. Walton upon all matters of business, which he understands much better than I do. Most likely the truth is that he wasn't half pleased about your uncle's will, and that may have made him a little short in his manner."

"He cannot be more displeased with it than I am," said Veronica disconsolately. "Did you ever before meet with the case of a person who had been enriched against her will and who would give a good deal to resuscitate the man who had enriched her for the sake of arguing the point with him?"

Lord Chippenham really couldn't say that he had, and seemed to be a little sceptical as to whether he was in the presence of such a case now. "You'll come to it," he declared encouragingly, with a subdued chuckle. "There are worse misfortunes than having more money than you know what to do with. As for argument, I suspect that if you could call my poor old friend Trevor back from his grave for that purpose, you would soon wish you had left him alone. You might argue with him till you were black in the face and you wouldn't convince him that he could possibly make a mistake. Argument was his strong point—or, at least, assertion was. I have never known Trevor's equal for dogged, persistent assertion."

"If he was capable of asserting that it was wise, or even reasonable, to leave an estate to me, he was capable of asserting anything!" Veronica exclaimed.

"He was," agreed Mrs. Mansfield, with melancholy conviction; "there can be no doubt that Samuel was capable of asserting anything and everything. Also the contrary of everything."

Lord Chippenham enjoyed his luncheon, as well as the conversation of the girl whom he had expected to be an uninteresting country bumpkin. Both were excellent of their kind, and both had that spice of originality which is so welcome to a man who is getting on in life and has seen and tasted most things. What tickled his fancy about Veronica was not so much her professed reluctance to become a rich woman (in which he scarcely believed) as the direct simplicity of her speech and her evident disinclination to accept advice from anybody. It was clear that, whatever might happen, she would take her own line and stick to it, regardless of the prejudices or reproofs of those about her, and this struck Lord Chippenham—who, it must be remembered, was no longer young—as a new departure in feminine eccentricity. However, if she was not eager for advice, she was very keen about acquiring information, and after luncheon was over, she returned unceremoniously to the dining-room, where he had been told he might smoke a cigarette, for the purpose of putting a few questions to him in the absence of an embarrassing third person.

"Oh, dear, yes!" answered the old gentleman, in reply to the first and most important of these. "Known him ever since he was a young subaltern; and a very smart young subaltern he was, too!—as fine a young fellow as ever stepped, I should say. Though his best friends—and he has any number of friends, let me tell you—would hardly pretend that he was likely to set the Thames on fire. But there's no satisfying some people. As for poor old Trevor, he was the kind of man who would have picked a quarrel with a stone wall. He would have quarrelled with me years and years ago, only I wouldn't let him; and you may depend upon it, my dear, that he would have quarrelled with you if you hadn't had the great good luck never to see his face."

"One always hears things too late!" sighed Veronica. "I would not have failed to force myself upon him if I had had the slightest suspicion that he entertained a misplaced affection for me. I suppose he is very angry and disappointed—Mr. Horace Trevor, I mean."

"Horace Trevor," answered Lord Chippenham, "is the best-tempered man in the world. Disappointed he may be—who wouldn't be, in his place?—but I doubt whether he is angry."

"I think," observed Veronica, "that I may very likely hand the Broxham estate over to him. It ought unquestionably to be his."

"Oh, you can't do that," said the old gentleman, laughing.

"You mean that he would consider such an offer an insult?"

"Well, yes; it would be an insult. Moreover, the property without the money would be rather a white elephant. A hundred thousand pounds sounds like a large sum; but I can assure you, my dear, that you won't find it so much as you may think. Poor Trevor was a wealthy man once; but he muddled away his money upon Church missions and Ritualist prosecutions and one thing and another, and land, as I dare say you know, is an expensive luxury in these days. I am by no means sure that I should care to take Broxham as a gift myself. However, that is neither here nor there. You and I may have our own opinion as to your uncle's wisdom and justice, but what has been done

can't be undone.   We must accommodate ourselves
to circumstances, that's all."

Perhaps the same notion may have suggested
itself at the same moment to both malcontents ; for
their eyes met, and they broke into a simultaneous
laugh.   The one method of pleasing everybody and
undoing what had been done was so ludicrously
apparent !   They did not, of course, carry indiscretion to the length of putting their thoughts into
words ; but Lord Chippenham presently departed in
so cheerful and benevolent a frame of mind that,
instead of making for the military club where he
was wont to enjoy an afternoon rubber of whist, he
turned in at another and somewhat smarter establishment, and inquired for Mr. Horace Trevor.

He was soon greeted by a young man, dressed in
deep mourning, whose appearance corresponded so
exactly with the succinct description of it given to
Veronica by Mrs. Mansfield that it is needless to
say anything more about him, except that he had a
remarkably pleasant smile.

"Still in London, General ?" this injured but by
no means despondent-looking individual said.

"Where else should I be ?" returned Lord Chippenham.   "If you know any better place than

London to be in at this impossible season of the year, you would do me a favour by letting me hear where it is. Besides, I've had matters of business to attend to. Come into the smoking-room; I want to talk to you."

And when he had ensconced himself in a comfortable armchair, he resumed : " Well, my dear boy, I have been lunching with Julia, and I have seen the heiress. All things considered, I think we may certainly congratulate ourselves. Strictly speaking, she isn't exactly what I should call a beauty ; but she is quite a lady, and she looks distinguished—yes, distinguished is decidedly the word. Clever, too, I should imagine, from the way that she talks, and quick at seeing things. In short, I'm convinced that she'll do."

" Oh, well—that's all right," responded the young man vaguely. " I am glad she is presentable, though it doesn't make much odds to me what she is like."

" My dear fellow, it makes all the odds in the world to you, seeing that she is your future bride."

" The deuce she is !" ejaculated the future bridegroom, staring blankly at his elderly mentor. " Who on earth told you that, General ?"

" Come now, Horace, don't pretend that you have

never thought of such a thing! It occurred to me as soon as I heard the will read, and so it did to Julia. Also, I suspect, to the young lady herself, who, I may tell you, is full of remorse for having cut you out."

"Oh, but that was no fault of hers," returned Horace hastily, "and I'm sure it never entered into my head to blame her in any way. I do trust you and Aunt Julia haven't been telling her that she ought to make amends by marrying me out of hand!"

"Do you set us down as born fools?" asked Lord Chippenham. "We aren't advocating indecent haste or anything of that sort; only we have the common-sense to see that the very best thing that could happen would be for you two to take a fancy to one another. And there's no reason that I know of why you shouldn't. Anyhow, you had better go round to South Audley Street and judge for yourself. Your Aunt Julia was complaining that you never go to see her now."

Horace Trevor had always been accustomed to address Mrs. Mansfield as "Aunt Julia," although in reality she was no more his aunt than the defunct philanthropist who had for so many years posed as his benefactor had been his uncle. He had a genuine regard for her and a grateful recollection of the frequent occasions on which she had undertaken to make his peace with her exacting brother. If he had been somewhat remiss about paying his · respects to her of late, this was because he did not wish to listen to lamentations over what could not now be helped. He had, of course, behaved like a fool; he had not been as conciliatory as he might have been; he had argued when it would have been just as easy, and a great deal more sensible, to have remained silent; he had not chosen to clear himself from imputations for which there had been very little real ground. But all that was over and done with, and what was the good of grumbling? Horace Trevor had always been of opinion that a man ought to preserve his independence; he had acted in accordance with his convictions (for he did not think that the payment of a few trifling debts by his uncle constituted any surrender of them) and he had been charged a heavier price than he had anticipated for the privilege. It only remained for him to grin and bear it, and, having an ample stock of good-humour to draw upon, he had accomplished both feats creditably enough. It certainly had not occurred to him that his misfortune was in any way remediable; still less had he contemplated rendering the late Mr. Trevor's will of none effect by the simple expedient of espousing Miss Veronica Dimsdale.

He felt no inclination to do so now—in fact he was quite determined not to do so; but Lord Chippenham's remarks had stimulated his curiosity a little, and he thought he would rather like to see the girl. He also thought that he would like to have an opportunity of making it clear to her that he was neither jealous nor covetous. He could well understand that the poor girl might be troubled with scruples, and he had no difficulty in realizing how Aunt Julia, with the best intentions in the world, would foster and encourage these. He pictured Veronica to himself as a simple little maiden, prone to be influenced by the suggestions of her elders and liable to be made unhappy by their displeasure. Now, one does not, if one is a good fellow in the main, want an unoffending girl to be made unhappy, even though she has stepped into a pair of shoes which were constructed for one's own feet and are likely to prove a trifle too large for her to wear with comfort.

On the following afternoon, therefore, Mr. Horace

went his way to South Audley Street, prepared to be very nice and friendly and to make everybody comfortable. He was far from being a conceited young man ; but he did flatter himself that he had the knack of setting people at their ease, and he had every excuse for so believing. As a matter of fact, he had pleasant manners, and, being fond of his fellow-creatures, was universally beloved by them. Even old Mr. Trevor had probably loved him, while sternly disapproving of him. At all events, there could be no question as to the sentiments entertained for him by Mrs. Mansfield, who jumped up when he was shown into her drawing-room, and greeted him with effusion.

"My dear boy," she exclaimed, "this *is* good of you! You know that Veronica Dimsdale is here?— staying in the house, at least. She isn't at home just now, I am sorry to say, which is most unfortunate. I wanted you so much to see her!"

"Well, I called to see you, you know," Horace remarked, with partial truth.

"Then all that I can say is that you have called to see a deeply disgusted old woman. I can't get over it, Horace. I really can't! And if we were not assured that purgatory is a fond thing, vainly invented, I should feel far from confident as to poor Samuel's state."

"Oh, you'll get over it," said Horace cheerfully; "I have already. Now let's hear about the heiress; the General was praising her up to the skies yesterday."

Mrs. Mansfield might have been imprudent enough to imitate Lord Chippenham in that respect if she had not detected a half-amused, half-apprehensive look in Horace's gray eyes which warned her against a too speedy betrayal of her schemes. As it was, she only said, "Oh, Veronica is charming. Not quite your style, perhaps; still, charming in her own way. I don't suppose it will be very long before some good man relieves me of all further responsibility for her."

"I don't suppose it will. Broxham is worthy of the attention of good men—not to mention bad ones."

"Ah! but I mean she will be married for her own sake. Tastes differ, you know. Of course, as I say, she isn't the sort of girl whom you would be likely to admire."

"I admire all sorts," declared Horace, who was not in the least taken in by this rather transparent diplomacy; "what makes you think that I shouldn't appreciate your Veronica? I thought you were so anxious for me to meet her."

"So I am," answered Mrs. Mansfield; "and so is she, poor thing! For naturally she cannot help feeling that you owe her a grudge, and she wants to be assured that you don't. I only meant to say that she is not at all like the class of young women with whom you are in the habit of flirting. The chances, I am afraid, are that you won't hit it off with her."

A few leading questions extorted from Mrs. Mansfield the confession that she herself had not as yet been brilliantly successful in hitting it off with her niece, whom she pronounced to be an incomprehensible mixture of docility and self-will.

"She has evidently been very well educated, but I doubt whether she has been very well brought up. She seems to have been accustomed to take her own way as a matter of course, and she won't discuss things. She either yields or she doesn't. More often than not, I suspect, she doesn't. When I told her that it wasn't quite the proper thing for her to go to the National Gallery this afternoon all by herself she wanted to know why. I said she might be insulted; but she declared that she really couldn't believe that, and off she went without more ado. Yet it stands to reason that she *may* be insulted."

"Oh, I expect she'll be all right," said Horace easily. "I have never been in the National Gallery myself, so I don't know what sort of people frequent that place of amusement; but I should imagine that they would be a highly respectable lot. Besides, I understand that she doesn't shine conspicuously in the matter of personal beauty."

Mrs. Mansfield said rather crossly that wasn't the question. "I suppose the General has been telling you that she is plain : he calls everybody plain who hasn't a little mouth and big eyes and a perfectly meaningless cast of countenance, like the beauties of his boyhood. Times have changed since then, and, unless I am very much mistaken, Veronica will have as many admirers as she can possibly want before she is much older."

The problem was to arouse Horace's interest and predispose him in Veronica's favour, without hinting at the possibility of his doing anything so eminently satisfactory as to fall in love with her. Mrs. Mansfield, more judicious than her fellow-conspirator, was alive to all the risks attendant upon plain speech, and when, on the expiration of half an hour, the young man, after glancing at his watch, said he must be off, she did not feel able to congratulate herself upon having advanced far towards the attainment of her purpose.

But in truth she had been more successful than she supposed; and the proof of this was that when Horace Trevor left South Audley Street, he bent his steps unhesitatingly in the direction of Trafalgar Square. He said to himself that really, when you came to think of it, it was a scandalous thing never to have been inside the National Gallery; and he also said to himself that it would be rather amusing to try and discover which of the dowdy females whom he expected to encounter there was Miss Veronica Dimsdale.

He was not, however, destined to increase his very scanty acquaintance with the pictorial art that day; for he reached his destination only in time to find that the doors were about to be closed and that everybody was coming out. He lingered for a few minutes at the entrance, watching the people as they emerged, and presently his eye fell upon a tall young lady in black, who, he at once made up his mind, must be no other than his fair supplanter. All doubt as to her identity was removed when, after looking about her in obvious perplexity, she addressed the attendant constable.

" I can't remember whether I ought to turn to the right or the left," she said, in a clear contralto voice.

" What address, m'm ?" the policeman inquired.

" That's just the stupid part of it !—the name has gone out of my head. It's South Something Street —Mrs. Mansfield's. But I suppose you wouldn't know who Mrs. Mansfield is."

The policeman admitted his ignorance and suggested reference to a Post-Office Directory, which, he said, would probably be obtainable at any neighbouring shop ; but at this juncture Horace judged it appropriate and permissible to intervene.

" I think you must be Miss Dimsdale, are you not ?" he said, stepping forward and taking off his hat. " I have just come from your aunt's house in South Audley Street, and I shall be very glad to show you the way there, unless you would rather that I called a hansom for you. My name is Trevor ; you have heard of me, I know."

The girl did not seem to be in the least shy or awkward. He noticed that, just as he had noticed already that her voice and manner bore the stamp of good breeding, and he was very much pleased when she held out her hand and exclaimed with a smile : " What a lucky chance ! You are the very person whom I most particularly wanted to see. I wonder whether you would mind walking part of the way home with me ?"

He made the only reply that could have been made, but his sincerity in making it was so unmistakable that Veronica felt drawn towards him at once. Indeed, there were not many people who did not take a liking to Horace Trevor at first sight. So these two paced along Pall Mall East, side by side, and the policeman, gazing benevolently after them, remarked to the doorkeeper that they made what he should call a 'andsome couple.

CHAPTER VI.

A FRIENDLY COMPACT.

"I AM sure," Veronica began, "you must heartily wish I had never been born. Don't trouble about protesting, for if I were you I should certainly feel just as you do; only I think you must admit that I am not in any way answerable for what has happened."

"Of course you're not," the young man declared.

"That is really my sole consolation. As I never even saw my uncle, and only once in my life had a sort of indirect message from him, I can't be accused of having exercised undue influence. I have always understood and always believed that he hated me for my mother's sake. I attached no importance to that message which came through Aunt Julia, and which was to the effect that I should get something when he died. In fact, it seems to be tolerably certain that at the time he only meant to leave me a small legacy. Oh, if he had but dropped down dead there and then how much better it would have been!"

" You aren't over and above grateful for benefits received," remarked Horace, with an amused side-glance at his companion.

" I have nothing to be grateful for. My benefactor threw me what he couldn't take away with him, not because I was myself but because I wasn't you. He has placed me in a most uncomfortable and embarrassing position, and it appears to me that he hasn't been even commonly honest. I suppose it was quite an understood thing that you were to succeed him, was it not ?"

" Oh dear no !" answered the young man. " I certainly expected that he would make me his heir, and so did everybody else ; but I can't say that he ever committed himself to a distinct promise. On the contrary, he threatened scores of times to cut me adrift if I didn't mend my ways."

" Were your ways so very bad, then ?" Veronica inquired.

" Upon my word I don't think they were ; but they weren't his ways, and so we had perpetual rows. I'm bound to confess that I wasn't very respectful to him; he used to talk such—well, he's dead now, and perhaps it wasn't really humbug. But it sounded uncommonly like it."

" He objected to your betting, I suppose."

"Oh, he objected to everything; you couldn't please him, and it wasn't much use to try. My own belief is that if I had joined the Salvation Army or become a total abstainer, he would have found something to object to in that."

" I dare say," observed Veronica reflectively, " you wouldn't tell me if he had had some more serious ground of complaint against you than I know of. Of course, I couldn't expect you to tell me. And yet it seems almost necessary that I should ascertain, by some means or other."

" I don't quite understand," said the young man, opening his gray eyes rather wide.

" And it is so difficult to explain! Perhaps you wouldn't mind just answering me in general terms if I asked you what sort of a life you have led— whether it has been what is commonly called a fast life, for instance ?"

Well, this was rather an odd question for a young lady to put, and although Horace was not offended, it made him feel unwontedly shy. Who is to know what young ladies understand by "fast"?

"You need not," Veronica went on, by way of setting him more at his ease, "feel afraid of shocking me. Girls know many more things than they are supposed to know, and I have read a good deal, and I am neither deaf nor blind, in spite of having lived all my life in a country parish. I don't want to catechise you; I only want, if I possibly can, to account for my uncle's conduct."

"I am afraid it would puzzle you to do that without having known him," Horace answered, laughing. "All I can tell you is that he was the queerest-tempered man I ever came across. Nothing that he did ever surprised me, and I wasn't at all surprised when I heard that he had altered his will after our last scene. However, I may say with a clear conscience that the worst offence I ever committed, in his eyes, was going to the races on a Sunday. I don't claim to have been a saint; but I haven't any reason to accuse myself of dissipation or hard drinking, or anything of that sort. In fact, I should think you could see for yourself by looking at me that I haven't."

Veronica, without concerning herself in the

slightest degree about the circumstance that they
were walking down Pall Mall in broad daylight, and
were attracting a certain amount of notice on the
part of the passers-by, scrutinised his healthy,
honest countenance and smiled at him.

" Thank you," she returned ; " it is very good of
you to have answered me so frankly, and I quite
believe what you say.   One can only conclude,
then, that my uncle was a sort of religious maniac,
and that he ought to have been deprived of the
management of his own affairs.   After all, the way
in which he treated my father and mother supports
that theory.   At the same time, I must own that
I myself have rather a prejudice against men who
are neither particularly bad nor particularly good—
men whose only object in life is to amuse themselves, and who never dream it is any business of
theirs to leave the world a little better than they
found it."

" Meaning me ?" Horace Trevor inquired.

" Ah ! I don't know. I might mean you. That's
just the question. I need hardly tell you that what
I should like to do would be to transfer this Broxham estate to you without delay; but, you see, it
is rather an important step to take. I think, per-

haps, I ought to satisfy myself first that you would try to make as good a use as you could of the property."

Horace burst out laughing.

" I beg your pardon," he said, perceiving that she was a little affronted. " I ought to be ashamed of myself for being so rude, and I am really grateful to you for your generous intention. Only, you know, the thing couldn't be done. In the first place, I couldn't rob you of your property ; and in the second place, a will which was made with the deliberate purpose of cutting me out of it couldn't be annulled."

" I shouldn't feel the smallest compunction on that score," Veronica declared. " We agreed that the man was not sane enough to make a will at all."

" Well, you said so; I don't remember agreeing with you. Uncle Samuel was quite as sane as most of us, I expect. Please don't bother yourself any more about the matter. It's awfully kind of you to have thought about me at all, and I'm very glad we have met. I don't see why we shouldn't be friends, do you ?"

" I should like nothing better than to be a friend

of yours," was Veronica's satisfactory response.
She added meditatively, after a moment, " In some
ways you remind me a good deal of Joseph."

" I often remind myself of him," the young man
replied gravely.   " That is, if you allude to the
Patriarch."

Veronica broke into one of her abrupt laughs.
" I was alluding to my young cousin, Joe Dimsdale," she said.   " He is very unlike you in appearance, because he has red hair, and he has never
dressed smartly, or wanted to dress smartly, in his
life ; but I think you would get on together all the
same.   You are fond of hunting and shooting, I
presume."

" I am very fond of hunting," Horace answered.
" Of course I do shoot, but I can't pretend to be
much of a shot.   However, nothing in the shape of
sport comes amiss to me."

" Nor does it to him.   Personally, I rather dis-
approve of sport, though I know that you would
justify it by the same arguments that he uses."

Like George III., who, in his simplicity, had
never supposed that the Bible stood in need of an
Apology, Horace Trevor had not until now thought
of seeking any justification for pursuits which have

received the sanction and approval of centuries. More in sorrow than in anger, he said he did hope Miss Dimsdale was not a Radical. " I haven't met a great many Radical women," he admitted, " but those whom I have come across have been more than enough for me. Awful beings, with their hair cut short or parted on one side, who made speeches from platforms and wanted to repeal—well, pretty well everything ! I am sure you can't belong to that hideous crew !"

Veronica replied that she did not at present contemplate making any change in the arrangement of her hair, but that she was endeavouring to bring an unprejudiced mind to bear upon all subjects. As she marched up St. James's Street she was proceeding to unfold, with considerable emphasis and appropriate gesticulation, the reasons that she had for doubting whether the slaughter of innumerable grouse and pheasants is an ennobling form for dexterity to take, when the approach of a tall, elderly gentleman, with a badly brushed hat and an exquisite Marshal Niel rose in his buttonhole, caused her to interrupt her harangue.

" Oh, here is Mr. Mostyn ! How delightful !" she exclaimed, holding out her hand to the new-comer, who greeted her in an affectionate, fatherly fashion and nodded to her companion.

"I have only just run up for a couple of days," Mr. Mostyn announced ; "please don't tell anybody that you have seen me."

There were a few people (and Horace Trevor chanced to be one of them) who thought that the great man's terror of being run after was just a trifle exaggerated, and that, in any case, there was no need for him to proclaim it quite so persistently as he did. But Veronica, knowing how great Cyril Mostyn really was, always took him with the utmost seriousness.

"I suppose we ought not to keep you standing on the pavement, where you are visible from the windows of all these clubs," she said anxiously. "Are you very busy, or could you, do you think, find time to look in at South Audley Street before you go back to the country ?"

Mostyn smiled, and shook his head. "I am afraid I can't manage it," he answered ; "to tell you the truth, I have every single hour engaged. Still, I might stay an additional hour or two in London if I were very particularly wanted. Am I ?"

Veronica, after biting her lip reflectively, felt unable

to assert that he was. What he meant, of course, was that he would be willing to give her his opinion of Horace Trevor. But she would not upset his plans upon so frivolous a pretext as that, and, after all, he probably knew nothing more about the young man than she herself did by this time. That reminded her of Horace's presence, which she had forgotten for the moment, and she said·: " Oh! by-the-way, you have met Mr. Trevor already, haven't you ?"

The two men made the customary inarticulate murmur and exchanged a few remarks referring to common acquaintances; after which there did not seem to be any special reason for prolonging the interview.

" I shall tell your uncle and aunt that I have seen you and that you are looking remarkably well," Mostyn said, as he took leave of Veronica. Then he added laughingly, in an undertone, " Don't be too hasty about solving that Hard Case in the manner that you suggested; such solutions are much more apt to result in blanks than prizes."

When Veronica and her escort had resumed their walk, the latter asked in a dissatisfied tone, " Do you like that chap ?"

" Oh, you certainly do resemble Joseph !" Veronica exclaimed; " he has asked me the very same question in the very same voice again and again. Yes, I like Mr. Mostyn very much, and I admire him even more than I like him. So would you, if you had read his writings."

" I have read some of them," Horace said; " they were a bit over my head, I suppose, for I must confess that I found them rather tough work. I have no doubt he is a genius, though. Only don't you think he is a little too conceited about it ?"

" Most certainly not," declared Veronica. " You can't be conceited when you are as big as that; vanity is one of the defects that belong to little people."

" Well, perhaps it isn't conceit then; perhaps there's some other name for the complaint when it attacks people of his size. But, whatever it may be, he has got it, and I can't help thinking that he would be improved by being cured of it. What did he mean by the ' hard case ' which he was so anxious to dissuade you from solving ?"

" I have a great mind to tell you," answered Veronica. " Yes, I don't see why I shouldn't; it may help us to be comfortable and friendly together if I do. He was only referring to a mild joke that I made just before I left home. I said my dilemma was very much like one of those which are published every week in *Vanity Fair*, and that the obvious way for the embarrassed young woman to make amends to the ill-treated young man whom she had ousted was to marry him. There is no harm in my mentioning this now, because, after talking to you, I feel quite certain that you will never wish to marry me, and though I like what I have seen of you very much, I am just as certain that I shall never wish to marry you. I shouldn't wonder if other people were to try to arrange a match between us——"

"Oh, they will," interrupted the young man; "they have begun already."

"I suspected as much, and really one can't blame them. But from the moment that we have made up our minds not to oblige them they won't be able to give us any annoyance worth speaking of. I hope you don't mind my talking like this. You were saying just now that you wanted to be friends with me, and I want above all things to be friends with you. In the absence of some mutual understanding and compact, that might be, made difficult for us, you see."

Horace laughed and answered, "All right." His acquiescence was a shade less cordial than it might have been, had he been less equivocally informed that Miss Dimsdale could not regard him as a possible husband. Certainly, he had no ambition to become her husband, while her proffered friendship was welcome to him ; but it is a part of the inborn perversity of human nature that we resent having our disabilities thrust upon our notice, however palpable they may be.

"And now that that is settled," resumed Veronica cheerfully, " let us discuss the question of the Broxham estate in an amicable, sensible spirit. Lord Chippenham says that the estate without the money would not be worth having ; but——"

"Oh, bother Lord Chippenham!" broke in Horace impatiently. "He may say what he pleases; but he knows as well as I do that it is absurd to talk about your resigning your inheritance. Please believe, once for all, that nothing — absolutely nothing on earth—would induce me to accept an acre of land or a shilling of money from you."

"Well, you needn't lose your temper over it," said Veronica reprovingly.

Horace declared that he had not lost his temper

—never lost his temper. At the same time, he must decline to be bullied ; and the last words he spoke to his companion, after leading her to Mrs. Mansfield's threshold, were : " Now mind, if we are going to be friends, there is just one subject which we must agree to avoid for the future."

CHAPTER VII

DOLLY CRADOCK.

MRS. MANSFIELD was delighted to hear that her niece had already made acquaintance with Horace Trevor, and even more delighted when the circumstances under which the acquaintance had been formed were related to her.

"What in the world could have taken Horace to the National Gallery, of all places!" she ejaculated.

"I don't know; I quite forgot to inquire," answered Veronica. "Now that you mention it, I suppose it was rather an improbable spot for a man of his tastes to be discovered in; though, to be sure, he was not in the building itself. He was standing on the steps outside with a policeman and a number of others."

Mrs. Mansfield smiled and abstained from further interrogation. Without being an especially pious

woman, she firmly believed in the constant inter-
vention of an overruling Providence, and it seemed
to her that Providence had taken this matter in
hand.

Most providential also did it appear to her that
from that day forth Veronica showed every dis-
position to be reasonable and tractable. At the
outset there had been no sort of certainty that the
girl would prove so; she had declined to discuss
further arrangements, had spoken as though the
question of her taking up her residence at Broxham
were too remote to be worth considering, and had
generally conveyed the impression that she meant
to do just exactly what she might think fit—a tone
which no girl with a properly qualified duenna ought
to assume. But now, as Mrs. Mansfield was very
glad to be able to inform Lord Chippenham, there
were distinct signs of a change for the better.

" Everything is working out much more satis-
factorily than one could have ventured to hope,"
she told her brother-in-law, about a week later.
" It has been decided that I am to go down to
Broxham with Veronica in the autumn, by which
time, Mr. Walton says, she can take formal possession of the place; meanwhile, she is to stay on here

as long as she likes. And I must say for her that she is not at all difficult to entertain. Perhaps I ought not to let her go about by herself quite as much as she does; but nowadays that sort of thing is the fashion, and it isn't as if there were the slightest fear of her coming to grief in any way."

"And what about our young friend Horace, who has already come to grief a good deal more than he has deserved?" inquired Lord Chippenham. "Is there any hope of his redeeming former false steps?"

"The very greatest hope, I should say," answered Mrs. Mansfield complacently. "He drops in, upon one pretext or another, almost every day, and Veronica and he talk together as if they had known one another all their lives. Oh, yes! I believe he is really smitten—though, between ourselves, I hardly expected such luck. Delightful as she is, and fond as I am of her, I can't call dear Veronica exactly pretty; and beauty—as you know as well as anyone—remains the one thing that men insist upon in women."

The experienced warrior chuckled and said, "Oh, we ain't so particular as all that; we can put up with trifling physical imperfections, if we are properly managed. Especially when it's a question of marriage, and when the lady has a substantial property of her own. Besides, I call Miss Veronica an exceedingly nice-looking girl myself."

Horace Trevor, as it happened, entertained a similar opinion, although Mrs. Mansfield would have been grievously disappointed if he had explained to her how it was that he came to be upon such excellent terms with her niece. He certainly could not and would not have paid such frequent visits to the house in South Audley Street, had there been a possibility of his motives being misconstrued by one of the ladies who dwelt there. As for the other, it was both agreeable and convenient to put her off the scent.

" I can't be thankful enough to you," he was pleased to tell Veronica, on one occasion, " for having taken the bull by the horns and said you would see me jolly well hanged before you would think of marrying me. If you hadn't done that, I should always have been afraid that you might suspect me of wanting to make up to you."

"Oh, I shouldn't have suspected you," returned Veronica, laughing. "You are not the sort of person about whom one could ever have suspicions

—they would be certainties one way or the other. I doubt whether you have it in you to deceive an intelligent child of five years old."

"Oh, well, come! I'm deceiving Aunt Julia and the General, at all events," protested Horace, rather resenting this charge of obvious integrity.

But in truth he was about as honest and simple a young man as could have been found in England, and that was one reason why Veronica had conceived a strong liking for him. The more she saw and heard of him (and she kept her eyes and ears open) the more she became convinced that his prospects had been marred without legitimate excuse and that he must, by some means or other, be reinstated in the position which was his of right. How this was to be contrived she could not yet determine; for she had reluctantly come to the conclusion that her original idea of retiring in his favour without more ado would have to be abandoned. She herself saw no reason why he should not accept a property that she did not want; but the objections to such a course appeared to be so cogent in his and everybody else's eyes that any further attempt to combat them would be a sheer waste of time. What she vaguely hoped for was that at some future date the transfer might be effected with less difficulty. All sorts of things might happen. She might, for instance, marry some rich man, who would not care about being burdened with an additional estate, and in that case, what could be more natural than that she should pass it on to her cousin? For she had already, by Horace's request and with Aunt Julia's approval, begun to speak of the young man as her cousin and to address him by his Christian name.

In those days—felt by her to be a sort of transition period, during which there was nothing to be done but to await the progress of events—Veronica found life pleasant enough. Although, in consequence of her recent bereavement, Mrs. Mansfield was declining all invitations, she did not deem herself precluded from receiving her friends, of whom she had a vast number; and it seemed to Veronica, who was accustomed to a very different method of existence, that there was a perpetual stream of people entering or leaving the house in South Audley Street. Many of these were politically or otherwise notorious. It was interesting to watch them; to listen to their talk and to note how extremely ordinary were the ideas to which they thought fit to give expression. Statesmen, fine ladies, artists, musicians—all these were to be met with in Mrs. Mansfield's drawing-room or at her dinner-table ; and Veronica, with a strong curiosity respecting the interminable Human Comedy and considerable natural aptitude for discerning its lights and shades, enjoyed scrutinising them and trying to discover what they were really like when off the stage. Moreover, if Aunt Julia's friends were not conversationally brilliant, or did not care to show themselves so, they had singularly pleasant, easy manners. They did not look half bewildered, half offended if you chanced to tell them what was in your mind at the moment, as the dwellers around Harbury Vale had been wont to do : their mental horizon was evidently less restricted than that which encircles country neighbourhoods ; added to which, they were exceedingly kind and anxious to do all in their power to amuse a raw rustic. The truth, no doubt, was that Veronica herself was amusing, besides being an heiress ; so that it would have been strange if she had not achieved popularity. As a fact, many people took a more or less disinterested fancy to her and were glad to afford her opportunities for enlarging her knowledge of contemporary social developments.

But of all her acquaintances she liked Horace. Trevor far the best. Now that they understood one another (or, at all events, understood one another with regard to one essential point), their intercourse assumed a character which was in every way agreeable, and even stimulating. That is to say, Veronica endeavoured to make her society stimulating to Horace, because she thought that he rather required a touch of the spur, and she found him a most docile disciple.

" Clever I shall never be," he confessed modestly one day, " and I'm not sure that I always agree with everything that you say ; but I'm quite sure that you are right in telling me that I ought to improve my mind, and I do read regularly every night now after I go to bed, until I fall asleep."

" And how long is that, upon an average ?" Veronica inquired.

" Well, it depends a little upon the author; but I'm getting on. I know quite a lot of things now which I should never have troubled my head about if you hadn't put me on the track."

" Any seeds of personal ambition beginning to germinate yet ?"

" H'm ! not many, I'm afraid. But I'm ready to

admit that I have wasted my life hitherto, and I would try to do something more useful with it for the future if I only knew how."

How, indeed, was he to render his future life useful to the community at large or of any great value to himself? An ex-cavalry officer who is too old to take up a new profession, and who has just money enough to live without a profession, is scarcely a promising subject. But Veronica's fixed idea was that he was to become a landed proprietor some day, and after that it would be comparatively plain sailing. For the time being, there was much satisfaction to be derived from the influence which she unquestionably exercised over this well-meaning young man, while it was at once a pleasure and a convenience to have his escort to theatres and other places of public entertainment.

"I don't think we show any disrespect to poor Samuel's memory by going to a theatre sometimes," Mrs. Mansfield said. "It is true that he wouldn't have approved of it, but then what *would* he have approved of?"

Not, it must be assumed, of a match between the disinherited Horace and the enriched Veronica ; and, since Mrs. Mansfield's object in going to the play was to foster that scheme, she reflected that she might as well be hanged for a sheep as a lamb. At the bottom of her heart she was old-fashioned enough to entertain some misgivings as to the propriety of showing herself at a burlesque or a comic opera within so short a time of her brother's death, but she told her conscience that the end justified the means.

What vexed her a good deal more than her conscience—a fairly well-trained one—was likely to do was the conviction which forced itself upon her one evening that she had adopted an unfortunate means of arriving at her end.

She was sitting, as usual, in the background of a box, the more conspicuous seats of which were occupied by Horace and Veronica, when the door was abruptly flung open to give admittance to a young lady in a sable-trimmed opera-cloak, who accosted her with the engaging *sans gêne* characteristic of a moribund century.

"How are you, Mrs. Mansfield? I saw you from the other side of the house, and I thought I would look you up between the acts."

"How do you do?" returned Mrs. Mansfield, in a tone of annoyed resignation. "I don't know how you could have seen me; but I suppose you mean that you saw Horace."

The new-comer laughed. "Well, yes," she answered, as she seated herself; "I divined you. It wasn't to be imagined that he could be at a theatre with a young person of unquestionable respectability and without his aunt. The young person is the heiress, I presume?"

She did not trouble herself to lower her voice, which was of a clear and rather hard quality. Both Veronica and Horace looked round, and the latter at once rose, holding out his hand.

"Have you come up for the season, Miss Cradock?" he inquired.

The lady addressed nodded. "Awfully sorry to hear of your sell," she was kind enough to say; "but I always warned you of what would happen if you didn't look out. What a duffer you were to let that old curmudgeon quarrel with you!"

Dolly Cradock prided herself upon her disregard of conventional usages. Most of us find it necessary to our comfort to pride ourselves upon gifts which we either do not possess or should be a great deal better without. This tall, well set-up and somewhat muscular-looking girl, who had a fine figure, a clear complexion, an abundance of bronze-coloured hair and a set of features to which not much exception could be taken, save that her jaw was rather too heavy for beauty, might have rested satisfied with what Nature and circumstances had done for her. Only in that case she would have been ordinary, and it must be assumed that she did not desire to be ordinary.

Horace, uncomfortably conscious of Veronica's vicinity, answered hurriedly, "Oh, that's all right. May I introduce you to my cousin, Miss Dimsdale—Miss Cradock."

" Didn't know Miss Dimsdale was your cousin," the irrepressible Dolly remarked, stretching out a tan-gloved hand to Veronica; " I always under-stood that you were one of those thrice-blessed mortals who have absolutely no surviving relations. Mrs. Mansfield don't count, because she is only your aunt by courtesy, and that doesn't give her the right to be discourteous, like some people's aunts. I wish all mine were in Abraham's bosom, I know !"

" My dear girl!" remonstrated Mrs. Mansfield.

But Miss Dolly was not in the habit of paying heed to remonstrances. She now proceeded to monopolise the conversation, criticising the first act of the play which they had witnessed in a spirit of candid impartiality, and displaying incidentally a remarkable acquaintance with the private lives of certain actresses concerned therein, until the entrance of Lord Chippenham created a diversion.

This left her free to devote her whole attention to young Trevor, to whom she said: "Well, and how are you? Bearing up pretty well?"

"Oh, I'm bearing up," answered Horace. "I say, I wish you wouldn't mind being a little bit particular about what remarks you make before Miss Dimsdale. She's—she's——"

"An *ingénue?* I shouldn't have supposed so, to look at her; she strikes me as being uncommonly self-possessed. Upon the whole, I rather like her looks, and I think I will cultivate her acquaintance. Just go round to the Framptons, who brought me here, and tell them I shall not be back until after the next act, will you? You can keep my place for me."

Horace obeyed not very willingly; for he knew that Dolly Cradock sometimes said outrageous things, and he had of late begun to form entirely new ideas upon the subject of what constitutes feminine attractiveness. But he had no need to be alarmed. Miss Cradock could suit herself to her company when she chose, and Veronica was almost as much pleased as amused by the frank speech of this fresh acquaintance. Dolly put a number of questions, obtained the information for which she asked, and gave in return a rapid and perfectly truthful sketch of herself and her belongings.

" Poor as church mice, and over head and ears in debt," said she. " But somehow or other we manage to hang on from year to year and keep more or less in the swim. How it's done I'm sure I can't tell you, but it *is* done. As for me, I am beginning my third season of anxious looking out for the rich man who ought to have married me, and who hasn't turned up yet. Your cousin, as you are pleased to call him, would have done very nicely, but, of course, he is out of the question now, poor fellow!" added Dolly, with a sigh.

" You can't make me feel more apologetic or more ashamed of myself than I do already," Veronica remarked.

" Oh, I don't suppose you owe him any apology— though I must say I envy you your good luck. Imagine waking up one fine morning to discover

that one was wealthy and entirely independent! If
I were in your shoes, nothing on earth should ever
induce me to marry."

"Very likely I never shall," answered Veronica;
"but as for being independent, that seems to be
scarcely possible. I can't live alone."

"Why not? Who is to prevent you, from the
moment that you are of age? All that you have to
do is simply to declare your intention of pleasing
yourself, and then let them rave. I sometimes
adopt that system, even though I'm not independent, and I find it answer very fairly well. Still, for
the present, you are not so badly off in being
chaperoned by Mrs. Mansfield, who is an old dear.
Mrs. Mansfield, I was just saying to your niece that
you are an old dear."

The recipient of this graceful compliment did not
look precisely enchanted; but Lord Chippenham,
who thought Miss Dolly great fun, bent forward,
laughing, to ask, "And what am I, please?"

"Oh! you're another; everybody knows that,"
the young lady answered. "Only you wouldn't be
any use as a chaperon; you are much too frisky and
flighty for such a position."

She went on chattering through the next act, to

which she paid no attention whatever, and when
Horace reappeared to conduct her back to her
friends, she not only took him away with her, but
retained him for the rest of the evening. This
behaviour it was which so exasperated Mrs. Mansfield that she could not help ejaculating, while she
and her niece were being driven homewards : " That
girl grows more and more vulgar every day! And
she has no business to be, for she is a gentlewoman
by birth."

" She promised to come and see me when she
could find time," Veronica remarked. " There is
something about her that I like. It is a pity that
she puts on that manner."

" It isn't put on ; she has never had any other
manner that I can remember. Although, as I say,
she becomes more objectionable as she becomes
older."

" Horace did not seem to object to her," Veronica
observed, after a pause. "Was there ever anything
between them ?"

"Oh *dear* no !" answered Mrs. Mansfield, with
unnecessary emphasis, " nothing beyond a mere
flirtation, such as he has had with dozens of others.
His going off with her as he did to-night was entirely

her doing, not his. And I always think that men who have had plenty of flirtations make the steadiest husbands. It is so much better that they should go through what has to be gone through in that way before than after marriage !"

" I dare say it is," agreed Veronica, laughing a little to herself in her corner of the brougham.

She was wondering whether Miss Dolly Cradock might not turn out to be a valuable ally. That that young woman would scruple to accept a wedding-gift of a fine estate did not appear likely, and if (as a slight change in the expression of her face when she began to talk about Horace had seemed to hint) she was really attached to him, and he to her, an arrangement satisfactory to all parties might yet be arrived at. This, however, was of course only a pleasing vision.

CHAPTER VIII.

COMPLICATIONS.

Miss Cradock did not lose much time about redeeming her promise to call in South Audley Street. She walked in, dressed in a riding-habit, one morning while Veronica was busy over the voluminous weekly epistle to which the denizens of Harbury Vale Rectory looked forward, and announced that she had come to lunch.

"It occurred to me all of a sudden in the Park," she explained, "that I would rather feed with you than with my own people, who are in a ruffled condition to-day owing to some row with our best tenant, who says he can't pay his quarter's rent; so I sent my old gee home and here I am."

"I am so sorry that Aunt Julia has gone to spend the day with an old friend at Hampton Court

Palace," answered Veronica. "Can you stand a *tête-à-tête* luncheon with me?"

"The very thing that I should like of all others," Dolly declared. "Mrs. Mansfield is a nice old woman, and I am very fond of her—much more so than she is of me—but on the present occasion I am quite clear that I prefer her room to her company."

And in fact it soon became evident that Miss Cradock would not have been nearly as interesting or as entertaining as she was in the presence of an elderly third person. During luncheon and afterwards she talked incessantly, and if her talk was for the most part purely egotistical, that was no drawback to it in the estimation of her hearer, who asked nothing better than to obtain some insight into the character of the potential Mrs. Horace Trevor. Many ladies, no doubt, would have been bored to death by Dolly Cradock; for loud, slangy girls, though less common than they used to be, are still common enough, and the type has ceased to be amusing; but for Veronica it had the advantage of novelty. Besides which, she had made up her mind to like Dolly.

"I have been thinking," she remarked, after

listening with some wonderment to a vivid description of certain riotous proceedings at a country
house in which the narrator had recently played a
prominent part, "that perhaps you might be persuaded to come down and stay with me at Broxham,
when we go there in the autumn. I am afraid I
can't promise that you shall meet people who will
throw tables and chairs at your head, because I
don't know any people of that kind, and probably
Aunt Julia's friends have more sedate habits; but
you might give us a trial. Horace says he will
come as soon as there are birds to be shot."

"You may expect me," was the decisive and
satisfactory reply, "and I won't do anything to
make you or your guests sit up. One can't play
the fool without assistance, and I'm sure I should
get none from Mr. Trevor, who seems to have
turned over a new leaf under your tuition. He has
a tremendous respect for you, you know."

Veronica laughed. "In what way has he turned
over a new leaf?" she asked. "Were the past pages
of his life such very bad reading?"

"Oh no; he has always kept pretty straight, I
believe. Only he used to be a cheery sort of fellow
and ready for any fun that was going. In a per-

petual funk of that canting old uncle of his, though.
And then to think of his having fallen out with the
old hypocrite and lost everything, after all! Doesn't
it just show what idiots men are?"

"Well, it shows that some men are very simple
and honest," answered Veronica. "I like Horace
all the better for not having been too subservient,
don't you?"

"No, I certainly don't," Dolly returned. "I see
no sense in cutting off your nose to spite your face;
I call that a very weak thing to do. However, he
has been sufficiently punished in all conscience, poor
fellow!"

These last words were spoken so ruefully, and the
drooped corners of Dolly's mouth seemed to intimate
in so unequivocal a manner that punishment had
not fallen upon Horace Trevor alone, that Veronica
was strongly tempted to make reassuring propositions
there and then. But she refrained. She was weary
of talking about surrendering Broxham and being
laughed at for her pains; if the thing was to be
done at all, it must evidently be done after some
slower and more diplomatic fashion. So she only
remarked, "Well, the least I can do is to serve him
a good turn, if I ever get the chance."

" I dare say he will give you the chance," observed Dolly, rather dryly.

" Oh, I don't mean in that way," said Veronica, replying to a speech which had not been made. " That arrangement can never come off, because we are both of us opposed to it. But there are other ways in which I may be able to help him when the time comes, if he is not too proud to accept my assistance."

" Are there ? I can't imagine what they can be. If he were a woman he might accept a big cheque— I should, I know, and say ' Thank you ' for it—but men aren't allowed to do such things."

With this statement of Miss Dolly's personal amenability Veronica had to rest satisfied; for now the dialogue was interrupted by the entrance of a visitor, who, it appeared, had insisted upon coming upstairs, notwithstanding Mrs. Mansfield's absence from home.

" I thought I might venture to ask for you," Mr. Mostyn explained, smiling pleasantly upon his young friend ; " it is so seldom that I have an hour to spare, and I undertook to bring you the latest reports from Berkshire."

Veronica said what was polite and veracious, was

duly informed that there was no particular informa-tion to be given respecting her relatives, and then introduced the great man to Miss Cradock. That the great man should never have heard of Miss Cradock before was, of course, not surprising; but it gave Veronica something of a shock to notice that the mention of her distinguished visitor's name elicited no further homage from Dolly than a blank stare and a slight bow.

"Mr. Cyril Mostyn," she could not help repeating under her breath, thinking that she might have been imperfectly heard.

"Yes; I know," answered Dolly, in a loud voice. And then, turning to the light of modern English literature: "Write a bit, don't you?" she asked.

"I must confess to having written a bit," Mr. Mostyn replied, much amused. "There are even moments when I am afraid that I have written a bit too much."

"Ah! I dare say. It must be a horrid grind, I should think."

"I often find it so," Mr. Mostyn admitted.

"Still, if you make money by it, it's worth doing, I suppose. I have sometimes thought of writing a sporting novel myself; sporting novels pay well, they tell me. But you don't go in for that sort of thing, do you?"

"No," answered the poet and critic, "I don't go in for that sort of thing. I am sorry to say that I don't possess the requisite knowledge."

"You don't look as if you did," Miss Cradock remarked candidly. "Well, I must be off. Veronica dear—may I call you Veronica, by the way?—I want a hansom."

She departed presently, after taking an affectionate leave of her hostess, whom she led as far as the door, with voluble assurances that she would come again soon.

Veronica felt bound to offer some apologies for her friend; but Mr. Mostyn did not seem to have been at all affronted.

"You think me a hero," he remarked, "because I have climbed to the top of the tree in a calling which you happen to admire; but the huntsman of the Quorn, whose name has probably never reached your ears, is an infinitely more important personage in the eyes of that young lady. And why not? I can do some things which he cannot do, but it is equally certain that he is my master in others."

"You might say the same of a chimney-sweep," observed Veronica.

"And in circles where chimney-sweeping is looked upon as a fine art I should hardly be accused of mock modesty. But I did not come here to talk about myself; I came to talk about you—or rather to ask questions about you. Do you know that it seriously alarmed me to see you walking in the street alone with young Trevor? All the more so because, when I mentioned the circumstance to your aunt Mrs. Dimsdale, she at once jumped to conclusions which she seemed to think a subject for congratulation. Your other aunt will naturally hold the same views; so that, unless you are prepared to stand very firm indeed, you may soon drift into a situation which I shudder to contemplate."

"There is no fear of that," answered Veronica. "I like Horace Trevor extremely, but I could no more think of marrying him than of marrying the Pope, and I am glad to say that he feels just in the same way about me. We talked it over the very day when we met you."

Mr. Mostyn raised his eyebrows and laughed. "It must be admitted that, for a poetess, you are an exceedingly practical person," said he.

"I only wish I were," sighed Veronica: "that is if a practical person means a person who knows how to put her wishes into practice. And don't call me a poetess, please; it hurts my feelings."

"The dictionary," returned Mr. Mostyn, "defines a poetess as a female poet, and a poet as one who has written a poem. I am ready to maintain in the face of the world that you have written a poem, and the fact that I recommend you to burn it is neither here nor there. We versifiers have at least one point in common with the phœnix, that if we ever rise to immortality at all, it is probably upon the ashes of our former selves that we do it."

"I shall never rise to immortality—nor even to notoriety—nor even to publication," said Veronica. "You know that quite well."

Mr. Mostyn smiled indulgently. "No," he answered, "I don't know that. I am a little afraid of it, I own, because, as I think I told you once before, riches are a terrible obstacle in the way of literary success. Your friend is quite right; we work for money, and if we didn't require money we should do very little work."

"You will never make me believe that your poems were written for sordid reasons," Veronica declared.

"Not altogether; but I should certainly have written more of them if they had proved more remunerative. As it is, I write more prose than I ought to do just because I find prose remunerative. After all, there are but two inducements to undertake the labour of composition—ambition and the necessity of earning one's daily bread in one way or another. The first is very soon satisfied; the other is almost sure to remain as a wholesome stimulus to literary men of small income until the end of their lives. Because I doubt whether even the authors of sporting novels ever realize sums large enough to be worth investing. For you, therefore, the question is one of ambition, pure and simple, and it will not take you long to discover that a woman with a large fortune may make herself famous by easier and speedier methods than by publishing a volume of poems."

"I have not the slightest desire to become famous," said Veronica impatiently; "I don't wish to waste my life, that is all. What have I done that you should deluge me with cold water in this way?"

"You have committed the almost unpardonable offence of being exceptionally lucky," Mr. Mostyn replied, laughing. "You really must not grudge your friends the small consolation of pointing out to you that your position has its drawbacks as well as its advantages. But so long as you abstain from the fatal step of espousing your so-called cousin, I shall not despair of you. Now, may I see what you have been scribbling since you came to London? For I know you must have been scribbling a little."

She had, in fact, been scribbling a little, and she was presently persuaded to submit her crude efforts to the scrutiny of a competent judge, who did not deal over-mercifully with them. He was, however, both kindly and straightforward—as, to do him justice, he always was, when treating of such sub-jects—and she had no reason to doubt his word when he assured her that she had made progress.

"You will make yourself heard of yet," he de-clared, "always supposing that you continue to think it worth your while to do so. And, between ourselves, it *is* worth while to do anything well, whether a reward in the shape of coin or celebrity is forthcoming or no."

That was more like the language that Veronica wished to hear; but when she reverted to the topic

of her burdensome wealth and her anxiety to shake
it off her shoulders, Mr. Mostyn had very little
comfort to offer her. It was evident that he had
no great faith in the sincerity of such murmurs;
he could not be brought to treat her grievance
seriously, and when he went away, he left a somewhat dissatisfied disciple behind him.

Later in the afternoon Horace dropped in, and
was pleased to accept a cup of tea. He had just
returned from Sandown, where he had had a very
successful day, he announced.

" I thought," said Veronica, in reproachful accents,
" that you were going to abjure betting. You can't
afford it, you know."

" Well, that depends," answered the young man
good-humouredly. " I can't comfortably afford to
lose, it is true; but I can do very well with a few
wins, and I feel quite like a capitalist this evening."

Veronica shook her head. " You might have felt
like a bankrupt, I dare say," she rejoined. " You
would have done much better to stay in London
and come to luncheon here. You would have met
Miss Cradock if you had."

Horace looked slightly uneasy. " Did you invite
her or did she invite herself?" he inquired.

"I believe she invited herself; but I was very glad to see her, and I hope to see more of her."

"She really is a good sort," Horace said half apologetically; "though you might not think so at first. Did she allude to current reports about us?"

"About whom? What reports do you mean?"

"Oh, I only thought she might have chaffed you; she is no respecter of persons, and I believe she would chaff the Queen if she got the chance. It's all over the place, you know, that you and I are going to be married."

"I did not know it was all over the place," answered Veronica, frowning thoughtfully; "I don't think I quite like it. Who can have been spreading such reports?"

"Oh, Aunt Julia and the General, I suppose. It doesn't matter, does it?"

"I don't like it," repeated Veronica. "We ought to be honest, I think, and I shall tell Aunt Julia to-night that she must not cherish any hopes of the kind."

"I trust you won't do that," said Horace; "you will let yourself in for no end of worry if you do. As it is, don't you see, we can be friendly and comfortable together; but there will be a finish to

all comfort as soon as Aunt Julia hears that we
don't mean business."

" I can put up with a little discomfort."

" I am not so sure of that, and I am quite sure
that *I* can't. Not with discomfort of that sort,
anyhow. I couldn't stay with you at Broxham, for
instance."

" Oh, you must come to Broxham. Miss Cradock
has promised to come."

" Ah ! that settles it, then. The Broxham partridges and pheasants will have to be shot by somebody else this year."

And although he was begged to be more explicit,
he refused to make any further revelations, merely
saying that it didn't signify, and talking persistently
about the people whom he had met at Sandown
until Mrs. Mansfield came in to relieve him of conversational difficulties.

Upon the whole, it seemed to Veronica that
nobody was at all inclined to help her out of her
own difficulties, which showed signs of becoming
increasingly complicated.

CHAPTER IX.

AFTER giving the subject full consideration,
Veronica decided against informing her aunt in so
many words that the project of undoing the perverse deeds of the late Mr. Trevor by means of a
matrimonial alliance was one which could never be
carried into effect. So far as she herself was concerned, she would greatly have preferred a straightforward course; but there were other people to be
thought of, and Horace's point of view was, after
all, comprehensible enough. He wanted to be upon
intimate, cousinly terms with the girl who had
supplanted him; but he did not want to be worried
and bothered, nor could he attempt to explain to
people incapable of understanding what he meant
that he was too much of a gentleman to fall in
with their ideas. He would, therefore, simply

absent himself—a thing which he must on no account be allowed to do. His expressed reluctance to meet Dolly Cradock needed no explanation, and it was entirely to his credit that, being now too poor to think of marrying, he should shrink from close association in a country house with one whom, under happier circumstances, he might have asked to share his fortunes. But it was clearly indispensable that he should visit Broxham and that he should meet Dolly there. Moreover, Veronica herself was too fond of him, and too sincerely interested in him, to contemplate the loss of his companionship with equanimity.

All these cogent arguments led her to make a compromise with her conscience. She did, indeed, tell Aunt Julia that she had been much annoyed at hearing of a ridiculous rumour to the effect that she was engaged to her cousin; but when Mrs. Mansfield rejoined, laughing, " Oh, my dear, that was certain to be said ; it isn't of the slightest consequence," she pursued the subject no further. It was not, she thought, necessary to protest that under no conceivable circumstance could such a rumour be justified by the event. Nor did she make any reply to her aunt's subsequent ejaculation of " Dolly Cradock, of course, has been repeating gossip to you! The truth is that she herself would have been only too glad to marry Horace when everybody thought that he had expectations.; but she would never have had the chance."

As to the accuracy of this latter assertion, Veronica had her own opinion ; but of course she kept it to herself. She likewise kept to herself all reference to the scheme of which an outline existed in her prophetic mind. At least Aunt Julia would not be able to say that any encouragement had been given to her own scheme, or that the persons concerned therein were responsible for its predestined failure.

Having arrived at that comforting conclusion, Veronica felt free to leave the future alone and enjoy the present, which was, in truth, very enjoyable. It is no bad thing to have plenty of ready money, to be allowed to do pretty much what you please and to be provided with entertaining and diversified society. When to this is added a congenial and deferential companion, in the person of a young man whom you have every hope of moulding in accordance with your ideas of what a young man ought to be, you must indeed be hard to please if you are not satisfied. During the week that followed Veronica was very well satisfied indeed. Everything seemed to be going as smoothly as could be expected; Aunt Julia was only too glad to keep her in London as long as she cared to stay; Mrs. Dimsdale, after some hesitation, had consented to let her defray the cost of Joe's agricultural tuition in the house of a gentleman-farmer, with whom it had been arranged that he should take up his residence; Mr. Mostyn looked in from time to time and spoke words of encouragement which were not, perhaps, to be taken too literally, but which were pleasant to listen to. The only question which gave rise to some harassing misgivings was whether, after all, Dolly Cradock was quite worthy of Horace. For there was no shutting one's eyes to the fact that Dolly was vulgar-minded, and increased intimacy with her rendered it impossible to imagine that her influence upon her future husband could be of an elevating nature. However, people must be allowed to choose for themselves in such matters, and Veronica felt tolerably certain that Horace's choice had been made. She was all the more certain of it because he took such pains to avoid meeting Miss Cradock, and because he could by no means be induced to talk about her. His one wish, apparently, was to spend as many hours as possible with the girl who had despoiled him of his inheritance, and, as may be supposed, it was not Mrs. Mansfield who was inclined to balk him of facilities for gratifying that wish. Veronica, knowing the true state of the case, could not help finding this a little amusing.

"What are you going to do to-morrow?" she asked him one Saturday afternoon when he was, as usual, sitting beside her at the tea-table, Mrs. Mansfield having (also as usual) retired into her own sanctum to write letters.

He replied that he didn't know; he had rather thought of looking in at Tattersall's.

"Ah, but I mean in the morning," said Veronica. "You ought, of course, to be going to church some- where; but I am afraid that you don't always remember to go to church. Why not come to St. Paul's with me? They are doing Schubert in F, which is well worth hearing, and perhaps the sermon may be worth hearing too."

"It *may* be; one never knows," assented Horace in a somewhat despondent tone. "But," he added more cheerfully, "I shall be delighted to go any- where with you. I find that I am beginning to like all the things that you like; so that there's a chance of my appreciating the music, ignorant though I am."

Appreciation can hardly exist without knowledge, but it is, fortunately, within the capacity of us all to admire what is beautiful, although we may not be able to specify our reasons for so doing; and perhaps it was because Horace Trevor's powers of admiration were very great that he thoroughly enjoyed the service to which he was duly conducted on the following day. He had never heard anything of the kind before—his previous experiences of Church of England services having been of a severely Protestant order—and, to tell the truth, he would have been puzzled to say at any given moment precisely what was taking place. Nevertheless, his emotions were stirred by the really exquisite rendering of a composition which cannot but appeal to everyone who has even an uncultivated musical ear : the pealing organ, the sweet treble voices, the subdued solemnity of the whole scene, the sense of space and remoteness in the heart of the vast city touched something within him which is generally known by the name of the devotional instinct. He said to himself that that sort of thing made him feel good—it may be that the occasional side-glances which he stole at his companion, who had evidently forgotten his vicinity, made him feel still better. In these days women are doing their very best to persuade us that they are neither better nor worse than we ourselves; but the illusions—if, indeed, they be illusions—of centuries die hard, and probably there will always remain a sufficient supply of simple-minded male creatures who, like Horace Trevor, will cling to the old theory of angel or fiend. And it was in very respectful and deferential accents that that young man addressed Miss Dimsdale when they left the cathedral together.

"I don't wonder at your being fond of sacred music," he said; "one can see that it is really sacred to you."

"Well, Schubert is," answered Veronica, who did not quite take his meaning; "but there are plenty of masses which are distinctly secular."

"You would say your prayers just the same, though, whether the music was secular or not," persisted Horace Trevor. "You were saying your prayers this morning."

"You weren't, then

The young man shook his head gravely. "Haven't done such a thing for years, I'm sorry to say. I had more than half a mind to begin just now; but then I thought, What's the use of making believe? It would only have been because of—because of you, don't you see!"

Veronica did not look as much shocked as he had expected her to be. "There is no use in making believe, certainly," she assented, with a slight laugh. "Do you mean that you are a sceptic?"

"Oh dear no," answered Horace, who, oddly enough, was himself quite shocked at the question; "only a sinner."

"I doubt whether you are a very heinous kind of sinner, and many excellent men are more or less of sceptics. There is Mr. Mostyn, for instance——"

"Oh, it don't matter what *he* is!" interrupted Horace; "I ain't going to take him for my model. What we all ought to be is what you are."

"How overjoyed Aunt Julia would be if she could hear you making such fantastic assertions!" exclaimed Veronica, laughing aloud. "Don't look so cross; I didn't mean to hurt your feelings, but really I am not what you take me for; it is only the music that has gone to your head. Besides," she added more gravely, "Christianity doesn't consist in saying prayers."

"What does it consist in?" Horace asked.

"I am going to lunch with one of the Canons, who ought to be able to tell you, if anyone can," answered Veronica. "Come and be introduced to him. He is a dear old man—a friend of Uncle John's, and he will be charmed to see you."

It did not occur to Veronica that there was anything startling or out-of-the-way in thus presenting herself at the house of her uncle's friend attended by a strange young man; nor was that eminent divine as scandalized as his wife would have been if he had had one. He was an amiable, hospitable and somewhat absent - minded old bachelor, in addition to being a distinguished theologian; Veronica's matter-of-course explanation that she had brought a hungry cousin with her appeared to him to meet all the requirements of the case, and he accorded a kindly welcome to Horace, whose spiritual hunger he was not invited to assuage in the course of the ensuing hour.

As for Horace himself, it must be owned that the unconventional character of the whole proceeding was not without a certain exhilarating effect upon him. There did, to be sure, exist a perfectly clear convention between him and Veronica, by virtue of

which he was where he was, and which entitled him
to say "*Honi soit qui mal y pense*" to all and sundry
whom it might concern. Still, he was, after all, a
young man and she was a young woman, while their
relationship was a fiction pure and simple. One
cannot entirely ignore such circumstances—unless,
indeed, one is so singular and admirable a mortal as
Veronica Dimsdale—and his mind dwelt upon them
a good deal more than upon religious difficulties
while he sat in the dim old dining-room, listening to
a conversation which related chiefly to matters of
which he had little personal knowledge. He was
surprised to find how much Veronica knew, how well
up she was in statistics and how capable of discuss-
ing the social problems of a great city with one
whose earlier and more active years had been spent
in an East-End parish.

"Do you know," said he, as they walked slowly
away from Amen Corner in search of a cab, "I am
beginning to think that the old chap who made a
rich woman of you was no fool. You will spend his
money more sensibly than he did, and a very great
deal more sensibly than I should have done if it had
come to me."

"I am glad you think so," answered Veronica.

She added, after a pause: "I only hope you will always do me the justice to think so."

"I shall always think that whatever you do is right," returned the young man, with conviction.

That sounded like a rather bold assertion to make; but Veronica said nothing in deprecation of it. She was conscious of being in some respects Horace's superior; she wanted him to look up to her, and indeed hardly saw how his future happiness was to be secured upon any other terms. She therefore permitted him, without contradiction, to praise her wisdom and unselfishness in glowing language until the sight of a solitary hansom caused her to interrupt his eloquence.

There are not too many hansoms to be met with in the City on a Sunday afternoon; so that you must take what you can get. Otherwise, Horace, who had not a Londoner's comfortable conviction that one horse is much the same as another, would probably have allowed that particular vehicle to pass unhailed. ·

"Mind his heels!" said he, as Veronica stepped in; and, sure enough, two resounding bangs upon the dashboard gave immediate justification for his warning.

"Is he going to kick?" asked Veronica, while Horace, after calling out the address to the driver, seated himself beside her.

"Yes, I expect so," answered the young man, who looked a little perturbed. "Shall we let this fellow go and walk on until we meet another?"

But Veronica answered, with a laugh, "Oh no! That would be too humiliating. Besides, a hansom isn't like a dog-cart. There would be a great deal of kicking to be done before we could be touched."

That was all very fine, but a hansom is an awkward conveyance to get out of; and they were no sooner off than Horace heartily wished that he had been more peremptory with his companion. The animal was young and fresh; he did not seem to be well accustomed to his work, and what was worse was that the driver was evidently afraid of him. After about five uneasy minutes — during which Veronica had been placidly contemplating the long vista of the Strand—the very thing happened which her more watchful neighbour had been inwardly dreading. A sudden gust of wind swept across the street, blowing a scrap of newspaper before it, just under the horse's nose. Up went the brute's heels, down went his head, and the next moment he was tearing off towards Charing Cross at a pace far too good to last.

It is never very pleasant to be run away with, but perhaps the most disagreeable time and place that could be selected for such an experience would be a London street on Sunday. Horses seldom bolt in a crowd, and even when they do, their career cannot last long ; but this excited beast had nothing in front of him, except a couple of omnibuses, with both of which he just missed colliding, and the only question was how far he would run before the inevitable smash occurred.

"Sit tight!" exclaimed Horace. But, indeed, there was nothing else to be done, unless it was to get down into the bottom of the cab, and this measure of precaution he was in the act of enforcing upon Veronica when he was abruptly shot out into the roadway, preceded by his hat, which somebody obligingly picked up for him. The horse had slipped and fallen heavily; the shafts were broken; the driver was lying insensible upon the pavement, and Veronica, neither frightened nor hurt, was stooping over the man, surrounded by a rapidly increasing crowd. Horace, after satisfying himself that she had really sustained no injury, was for withdrawing her from the throng at once, but to this she could in no wise be induced to consent. Not a step would she stir until a couple of policemen had arrived upon the scene, and the horse had been got upon his legs again, and a stretcher had been procured for the luckless cabman ; nor would anything serve her then but to join the procession which was presently set in motion for Charing Cross Hospital, where she insisted upon awaiting the verdict of the house-surgeon, which was, fortunately, a favourable one. Then she took the name and address of the sufferer, said she would visit him again on the morrow, and promised that his wife and children should be provided for as long as might be necessary.

All this was doubtless no more than what obedience to the dictates of common humanity enjoined ; but there is no known method of determining what people actually are or do. They and their conduct are, for all practical purposes, what they appear to us to be, and it appeared to Horace Trevor that Miss Veronica Dimsdale was a woman of quite extraordinary courage and benevolence. On the way to South Audley Street he told her so, with rather more emphasis, perhaps, than the occasion called for; insomuch that she laughed heartily at him, although his praise was not displeasing to her.

"I am getting my share of compliments to-day," was her concluding remark, as she took leave of him on the doorstep. "At this rate, I shall soon realise your ideal of absolute perfection. And yet if I ever beg you to grant me a small favour the chances are that you will regret your inability to do what you are asked."

"Try me," said Horace.

"Well, perhaps I will some fine day. Now I must go in and relate my adventures to Aunt Julia, who will at once add a story to her castle in the air upon the strength of them."

Horace walked off in a meditative mood. He himself was unconsciously laying the foundations of a castle in the air, and had been so occupied since the morning; but, to do him justice, he no sooner discovered what he was about than he promptly stopped operations.

"Hullo!" he exclaimed aloud, "this will never do! A nice peck of trouble I shall land myself in if I don't look out! Luckily, it isn't too late to pull up, and pull up I must before I begin to run down the hill. Henceforth, my dear Veronica, we won't see quite so much of one another."

He paced on for some little distance, with a rather rueful countenance, and then relieved his feelings by a second audible ejaculation—for he was crossing Grosvenor Square at the moment and there was nobody within hearing—

" What beats me is how the General, who has a pretty quick eye for good looks, can have described her as no beauty! If he had seen her sitting in that hansom cab, as cool as you please, with death staring her in the face, he would have altered his opinion, I suspect. However, it's nothing to me whether she is lovely or plain. No! if there is a certain fact in the world it is that that must never be anything to me."

CHAPTER X.

IT is very hard luck to lose your heart to a girl whom you cannot possibly marry : worse luck by a long way—such, at least, was Horace Trevor's opinion—than to lose a fortune through her. But he consoled himself with the reflection that he had not lost his heart yet ; he was only in some danger of doing so. As to the impossibility of his ever marrying Veronica, that was manifest. The thing was impossible, not so much because he had honourable scruples about enriching himself in such a way as because she would most assuredly refuse him were he insane enough to propose to her. Moreover, she would consider, and rightly consider, that he had played her false. A compact had been entered into, and it must not be departed from, happen what might.

What seemed more than likely to happen, unless immediate steps were taken to avert the calamity, was that her natural acuteness would enable her to detect a state of things which ought to be concealed from her. Horace, therefore, made up his mind to take immediate steps ; and perhaps it was by way of inaugurating a fresh departure that he betook himself forthwith to South Kensington to call on Lady Louisa Cradock.

On arriving at his destination, he found, as he had anticipated, a number of hilarious persons of both sexes gathered together ; for Lady Louisa was always at home on Sunday afternoons, and her daughter's friends were accustomed to make themselves so under her roof. She herself was a faded, careworn little woman, whose dress resembled her carpets in respect of being threadbare and who never exerted herself to entertain anybody. It was Dolly's business to do that, and Dolly was generally considered to be immensely entertaining. Horace himself had always hitherto concurred in the general opinion ; but then Miss Dolly had not hitherto been entertaining at his expense, as she now saw fit to be.

" Well, you *have* got a nice pair of broken knees

on you!" was her jocose greeting. "That ought to be a good twenty pounds off your value—which isn't what it used to be, anyhow."

Horace glanced down, and for the first time perceived two large muddy patches upon his trousers, which he vainly attempted to rub off with his hand.

"Never mind," resumed Dolly, "it looks respectable, after all—shows you have been to church. One of those Ritualistic places of worship where there are too many services to leave time for scrubbing the floor, I suppose. And I'll lay two to one in half-crowns that I name the person who took you there. What a pity that you should have taken to pious practices too late in the day! But perhaps it isn't too late—eh?"

"Piety hadn't anything to do with it; I've been pitched out of a hansom," answered Horace rather gruffly; for he was conscious of an amused and rather inquisitive audience, and he did not at the moment care about being chaffed upon the subject of his intimacy with Miss Dimsdale.

But of course there was no escape for him. He was made to give a full account of the manner in which he had spent the day, and Dolly's comments on his narrative, if humorous, were not of a nature to please him. He began to see what had not struck him before, that he ought not to have exposed Veronica to the more or less ill-natured gossip of lookers-on. Mrs. Mansfield, who anticipated an engagement, could afford to allow him privileges which he had had no business to claim ; but since there was to be no engagement, and since he had known all along that there was to be none, his conduct had certainly been thoughtless. Now he had to submit to the banter of Dolly Cradock and her friends, his denial that there was anything in the shape of a flirtation between him and the lady whom he persisted in calling his cousin being naturally taken for what it was worth. There had, however, been at one time something almost more pronounced than a flirtation between him and his present tormentor, and in his simplicity he could think of no better way of stopping her mouth than attempting a renewal of it.

"I think *you* at least might spare me this sort of thing," he took occasion to say to her reproachfully in a low voice, under cover of the temporary diversion created by the entrance of a fresh visitor.

Dolly shrugged her shoulders and made a grimace.

" Don't apologise," she returned. " The wind has changed ; you are quite right to shape your course accordingly."

" But I am not shaping it in *that* direction, and I wish you wouldn't talk as if I were. I know well enough that the wind has changed, and I can't— well, I can't look forward to things which I might have looked forward to once upon a time ; but I do assure you that neither my cousin nor I are dreaming of what you mean, and I don't want to be annoyed by false reports."

" But really, my dear friend, it doesn't make the slightest difference to me whether the reports are false or true."

" I suppose not," answered Horace, with a rather hypocritical sigh ; " only it would be kind of you to discourage them. At this rate I shall soon have to give up all my female friends. Some of them I mustn't visit lest I should be supposed to be a fortune-hunter, and others I have felt bound to avoid because I have become such a hopeless detrimental."

The odd thing was that this palpably insincere explanation of the fact that he had latterly neglected his duty towards a certain lady friend was accepted.

If Dolly Cradock had really wished to marry her quondam admirer, she might have been less easily convinced ; but she had no idea of linking her fate with that of a hopeless detrimental. Her only feeling in the matter had been one of slight mortification that another should bear away what had once been a prize, and she was not unwilling to make believe a little for the sake of securing a cheap triumph. So she said compassionately—

" Poor fellow ! Well, you shan't be accused again of wanting to do the only sensible thing that there is to be done, under the circumstances. But it isn't necessary to cut old acquaintances because you yourself have been unfortunate enough to be cut out of your inheritance. Give us credit for not being so desperately eager to jump down your throat, and look us up sometimes, as you used to do before the superior Veronica took you in hand and tried to elevate your taste."

It was close upon dinner-time when Horace quitted a house which he had esteemed in former days to be one of the cheeriest in London. If his taste had now become so elevated that its inmates and habitués had ceased to attract him, that, he felt, was scarcely a matter for self-congratulation.

He must seek amusement somewhere or other, but certainly not in South Audley Street; and the worst of it was that he doubted very much whether amusement was obtainable for him elsewhere. However, he was determined to try—the more so because he had a genuine liking for Dolly Cradock, notwithstanding her lack of refinement.

During many successive days, therefore, both Mrs. Mansfield and Veronica were made to wonder what in the world had become of him. The former ended by growing seriously uneasy; the latter, though a little piqued, said to herself that nothing was more easily to be accounted for than his absence. Of course he had his own friends and his own pursuits, neither being identical with hers, and if she had been able for a time to wean him from these, that only showed how good-natured he was. Besides, she really did not want to have him always following her about. Much as she liked him, she could quite conceive the possibility of having too much of his society and could quite forgive him for having had, apparently, too much of hers. This was what she said to her aunt, who suspected that there had been a quarrel and whose persistent queries were sometimes troublesome to evade.

Fortunately or unfortunately, Mrs. Mansfield had
other sources of information, from which she learnt
that Horace had been seen every morning riding in
the Park with Dolly Cradock; and, putting two
and two together, she came to the conclusion that
the best thing she could do was to write a somewhat peremptory note requesting the young man
to come to luncheon, as she had matters of business
upon which she wished to consult him. The sum-
mons was dutifully obeyed, and the matters of
business (which referred to the investment of some
money, a subject as to which Horace's opinion was
of no value whatsoever) did not take long to dispose of. Then the good lady, who had listened to
his observations with a great show of deference and
attention, said she must write to her bankers and
brokers at once, and begged him to talk to Veronica
in the drawing-room for a few minutes while she
finished her letters.

Now, Veronica, as it chanced, was not best
pleased with the way in which he had behaved
during luncheon. Certain symptoms—a visible em-
barrassment of manner, an unnatural loquacity, a
careful avoidance of her eye—which had appeared
to his hostess to indicate nothing more than that

nervous apprehension which a young man who has unhappily fallen out with the girl of his heart may be expected to display, were open to quite another interpretation, and it was in this latter light that Veronica had been disposed to view them. Consequently, her features did not relax when he came into the room, smiling, and said—

" I've been sent in here to talk to you. Poor old Aunt Julia! she ain't a diplomatist of the very first water, is she ?"

" As far as that goes, I don't know that you are quite in a position to criticise her," Veronica observed dryly. " Your thoughts are generally written upon your face in tolerably plain characters."

Horace came to a standstill and said, " Oh, I hope not !"

" I would not entertain that hope if I were you ; it will never be anything but a very forlorn one. After all, there is nothing to be ashamed of in having a speaking countenance, and I have always liked you for being unable to conceal your thoughts. At the same time, I wish you did not have such thoughts !"

The young man, being now quite sure that his

secret had been detected, dropped into a chair and answered sorrowfully, "I am awfully sorry, Veronica, but I can't help them, you know."

" Can't you ?   Well, I suppose it is natural to men to be vain and—horrid.   For the last two or three days I have had a dawning suspicion of what it might be that kept you from coming here as usual, and now I know.   I shouldn't be telling you the truth if I didn't say that I am disappointed in you.   However, we won't quarrel over it."

" I wish with all my heart that you hadn't guessed; but don't you think I was right to stay away, Veronica ?" pleaded poor Horace humbly.

" I certainly do not think that your reason for staying away was a good one, and I can't understand why you should harbour delusions which I have never done anything at all to encourage.   You don't seem to have much belief in my word ; but surely you might believe that I am speaking the truth when I assure you that, if you were the only man in the world, I should not marry you !"

" Since you say so, no doubt it is so.   Thank you for putting the case in such a forcible way," answered Horace, with a shade of resentment in his voice; for indeed assurances of that kind can hardly be made palatable to their recipient, however salutary they may be.

" Very well, then; let us drop the subject, and begin again where we left off. It is most disagreeable to be forced into saying what I have had to say; but you will allow that you have only yourself to blame for it. You ought to have known better."

Horace ruefully admitted that he ought. " But I don't know about beginning again where we left off," he added ; " it isn't so easy to forget things, even though one may be quite willing not to mention them any more."

" Oh, nonsense !" returned Veronica, laughing. " If I am ready to forgive and forget, it can't be asking too much of you that you should do the same. Especially as you have nothing on earth to forgive. You have made a mistake, and you confess that it was a mistake : that is enough. Let us consider the whole incident wiped out and say no more about it. Now tell me what you have been doing with yourself all this long time."

Horace did his best to appear friendly and unconcerned; but it was scarcely within the power of mortal man to help feeling a little bit sore, or to

help showing that he felt so. He had not expected
Veronica to divine what he himself had ignored up
to the moment of their last parting ; yet, since she
had divined it, a little more sympathy and a little
less *brusquerie* would not have been out of place, he
thought. Why was he to blame for having fallen
in love with her ? If he had so far forgotten their
respective positions as to propose marriage to her,
that would have been quite another thing. So the
dialogue that followed did not at all resemble previous dialogues held between him and Veronica, and
perhaps, in the course of it, he dwelt rather more
than was absolutely necessary upon the circumstance that he had seen a great deal of the Cradock
family of late. When a man has just been informed that if he were the sole representative of
his sex upon the surface of this planet, one woman
at least would never deign to look at him, he is
not unnaturally disposed to hint at the existence of
other women less hard to please.

Veronica, for her part, seemed to be, and indeed
was, much interested in all that he had to tell her.
She spoke with magnanimous approval of Dolly
Cradock, encouraged him to be more communicative and shook hands with him warmly when Mrs.

Mansfield came into the room with her bonnet on, which he took as a signal for him to rise.

" I hope," said that well-meaning lady, as soon as he had departed, " that you have contrived to put poor Horace into better spirits ; he looked quite ill and unlike himself at luncheon, I thought."

" Oh, I don't think there is very much the matter with him," answered Veronica, laughing, "and I am sure he will always be like himself. He has no sort of aptitude for being like anybody else."

Nevertheless, she confessed to herself, after she had begged to be excused from accompanying her aunt to a musical tea-fight, that she had not until now known exactly what Horace was like. She had supposed him too simple, too unsuspecting, above all too modest to fall into so preposterous an error as that to which she had understood that he had owned ; it did not increase her respect for his intelligence that he should have deemed it necessary to protect her from a wholly imaginary danger and absent himself lest his fascinations should prove too much for her fortitude.

" But, never mind !" was the reflection with which she finally dismissed this unpleasant episode from her thoughts : " I told him I would forgive and forget, and I must be as good as my word. I think, too, that I must have made him feel rather foolish. The main thing is that we are still friends, and, with ordinary luck, I ought to be able to arrange matters so that he shall be squire of Broxham before another year is out. When once that business has been settled, we can go our several ways, and I dare say we shall not meet often again ; for, somehow or other, I don't feel as if I should ever care to be very intimate with Dolly Cradock."

CHAPTER XI.

ENOUGH OF IT.

IF we were all of us able to perceive the tolerably obvious, the world in which we live would proceed along its appointed course much more smoothly than it does; wars would be less frequent, party government would have to be abolished, lawyers would have to join the ranks of the unemployed and harmony would reign in private life. But, on the other hand, existence would perhaps become a somewhat dull and uneventful business; and this thought may serve in some measure to console people like Horace Trevor and Veronica Dimsdale, who contrive to misunderstand one another where no misunderstanding ought to be possible. Veronica might have had sense enough to realize how extremely unlikely it was that a young fellow whose natural modesty she had recognised from the first should be seized all of a sudden with the panic which she had imputed to him, while Horace should have known that, if she had really guessed the state of his feelings, she would have dealt more gently with him; but neither of them was capable of bringing an unbiased judgment to bear upon the circumstances, and thus they became estranged, notwithstanding their ostensible amity. When they met, they were to all outward appearance as good friends as ever; but they did not very often meet, nor was their intercourse of the old confidential kind.

"Give them time," the experienced Mrs. Mansfield said to her brother-in-law, who was growing impatient and who wanted to know what the deuce the young folks were waiting for; "they have had a little tiff, but they have made it up again, and we can't do better than leave them to play out their comedy in their own way. After all, it is early days yet."

"I don't know what you call early days," grumbled Lord Chippenham; "I know we are getting within sight of the time when we shall all have to leave London, and I want this business to be settled before the end of the season."

Mrs. Mansfield also would have been glad to be

relieved of further anxiety upon the subject ; but she had found out that Veronica was not a very easy person either to lead or to drive, and she did not want to spoil a promising scheme by injudicious meddling. The wisest plan, she decided, was to allow her niece plenty of liberty, to ask no questions and make no visible efforts to attract Horace to the house. It might likewise not be amiss to arouse the young gentleman's jealousy a little should such an incentive prove manageable. With this end in view, she neglected no opportunity of throwing the heiress into the society of those who were only too eager to make the acquaintance of heiresses ; and if this stratagem was not crowned with any great success, so far as Horace was concerned, it had at least the effect of causing Veronica to appreciate him more highly by comparison with his neighbours.

" What would become of one's faith in human nature if one were condemned to spend all one's days in the fashionable world !" she mentally ejaculated, after an elderly widower and two gay young bachelors had displayed the most unbounded faith in her own nature by kindly offering to share their fallen fortunes with her. " Not one of these men can know anything at all about me, except that I am

rich, and evidently that is all they care to know.
The more I see of these people the more I admire
Horace for having remained an honourable little
gentleman in spite of them. The only wonder is
that, instead of sheering off when he took it into his
silly head that I was becoming too fond of him, he
didn't hasten to profit by such a stroke of good fortune !"

But Horace, for weal or for woe, had ceased to be
among her intimates, and—whether in consequence
of that fact or not—London society had ceased to
interest her. She told Mr. Mostyn, who had been
amiably instrumental in making her known to
sundry celebrities who were not precisely fashionable, that she was tired of it all and wanted to be
out of it.

He laughed, and replied, " I have been waiting for
some time to hear you say that. It is necessary to
look closely into things ; but, unfortunately, very
few things will bear looking into, and very few
people are as big as they appear to be from a distance. Never mind ! there is a good time coming,
when you will be able to survey all this as a whole,
and when it will furnish you with ideas—inspirations
even."

But Veronica did not see how it could possibly do that. All that can be said about the pettiness and cynicism of the so-called great world and the littleness of great men has been said scores of times already; her soul yearned for the green meadows and the pleasant, wholesome sights and sounds of the Thames valley; she was, in short, thoroughly homesick, and painfully aware that she no longer had a home.

It was while she was in this dissatisfied frame of mind—which was all the more dissatisfied because she could not have said precisely what was wrong with her—that she was taken, one afternoon, by her aunt to call on Lady Louisa Cradock. She had already exchanged visits and a few unmeaning words with that rather dowdy and forlorn lady, of whom she had retained no distinct impression, and when she was ushered into a drawing-room where several old women were seated, she did not feel it her duty to take any part in their commonplace conversation.

Mrs. Mansfield, whose income had not suffered from agricultural depression, who could afford to employ an expensive dressmaker and was a good deal more *dans le mouvement* than they were, cheered them up with her brisk talk, reminding them, it may be, of happier days gone by and exciting their interest by personal anecdotes, picked up in circles which they had ceased to frequent. Veronica sat a little apart, scarcely listening to them, yet moved with a vague pity for the poor old souls, who had lost all that they really cared for on earth with the loss of those two most essential advantages, youth and money. Their voices, as well as their remarks, were pitched in a minor key. They seemed to feel —what was probably the case—that they had no further *raison d'être*. Soon they would be dead and buried, and there was no reason to suppose that any one of them would be missed. Meanwhile, they pricked up their ears and a certain animation became perceptible upon their withered countenances when they heard that the Duchess of A had publicly cut Lady B, on account of her behaviour with the Duke ; or that Lord C was said to have actually married Miss D, the notorious music-hall singer.

It was very hot weather. The windows were open and the sun-blinds drawn down. Outside there was an uninterrupted roar of distant traffic, which some-how deepened the effect of profound melancholy produced upon Veronica by this tittle-tattle. The world is so tremendously busy, and time is rushing on at such a headlong pace: those who are not hard at work are at least hard at play, and to be stranded on the brink of the flowing current seemed to her to be about the saddest thing that could happen to anybody. It was terrible to think that a day might come when she too would sit, useless and forgotten, in a drawing-room, with nothing better to do than to gossip about people whom she did not even know, save by repute. Suddenly a loud outburst of laughter, followed by a babble of young voices, rose from immediately beneath her feet.

" That won't be quite so depressing as this, anyhow," she thought; and, jumping up, she said to Lady Louisa, in her abrupt way, " I am going downstairs to see Dolly for a few minutes; I can hear that she is at home."

Veronica had already more than once visited Miss Dolly in the den which that young woman had appropriated for her exclusive use, and which would have probably been her father's study if Mr. Cradock had not been a submissive old gentleman who spent most of his time at his club. She made her way thither unhesitatingly now, having received a friendly assurance that she would always be welcome, and opened the door without knocking. Then she paused on the threshold, wishing that she had been less precipitate, and angry with herself for having done a stupid, clumsy thing.

The air was thick with blue clouds of cigarette-smoke; Dolly herself, lolling in a deep armchair, was smoking; so were two smartly-attired young men, one of whom was seated upon the table swinging his legs; so was a third, who, as soon as he recognised her, pitched his cigarette out of the window and looked caught. The laughter which she had heard when she turned the door-handle had been quenched by her entrance. The two strangers were staring at her interrogatively, and Horace, with whom she felt quite irate, had the appearance of wishing very much to follow his cigarette. But Dolly was not easily put out of countenance.

" Come in," she said ; " sit down and make yourself comfortable. No use to offer you tobacco, I suppose. Now, Tommy, go on with your story."

The young gentleman addressed slid off the table and began to look for his hat. " Tell you the rest some other day," he answered ; " it's about time for me to be off now."

It took him some minutes to make his adieux and

to murmur a few parting jocularities in Miss Cradock's ear, while Veronica, who had not sat down and was feeling far from comfortable, awaited his exit. But at length he went away, taking his friend with him, and then the intruder was able to apologise.

" I am very sorry to have broken up your party," she said, in a voice which she could not keep from sounding constrained and annoyed. "I ought to have known better than to bounce in upon you in that way, and I will never do such a thing again, I promise you."

" Oh, we don't mind, if you don't," returned Dolly, with a laugh and a glance at Horace, who, for his part, seemed to mind a good deal; "the only misfortune is that you have been shocked. Not so shocked as you would have been if you had heard the end of that story; still, quite shocked enough. What can I say? There is really no blinking the fact that I do enjoy a cigarette occasionally."

" It would be no business of mine if you enjoyed a pipe," returned Veronica, not very civilly; "but I wish I had not prevented you from enjoying the conclusion of your friend's story. As you know it already, you had better impart it to Mr. Trevor, who must be dying of curiosity. I will go upstairs again and join the old ladies."

Of course she was not allowed to do that. She was made to sit down and talk until Mrs. Mansfield sent a servant in search of her, and during the ensuing ten minutes she recovered her equanimity sufficiently for all needful purposes, so far as Dolly was concerned. But Horace, much aggrieved at having been spoken of as "Mr. Trevor," had effected his escape without so much as shaking hands, and what added not a little to Veronica's vexation was that she should have shown in so unequivocal a fashion how displeased she was with him. What right in the world had she to be displeased with him ? Why should he not smoke cigarettes and listen to highly-flavoured stories in the company of one whose tastes were in harmony with his own, and who, it was to be hoped, would some day bear his name ? "I could not have behaved more like an utter idiot if I had been jealous of the girl ! And no doubt he thought I was," reflected Veronica furiously, as she sat beside her aunt in the carriage and endeavoured to preserve an aspect of unruffled calm.

She did not mention that she had seen Horace,

not wishing to be questioned upon the subject, nor did Mrs. Mansfield ask her whom she had met downstairs. It was rather a relief to be gently remonstrated with for having quitted the drawing-room so abruptly and to be told that Lady Louisa had thought it odd of her.

"It is best not to be odd," Mrs. Mansfield said; "people notice it, and they don't like it. In Dolly Cradock's case it doesn't perhaps matter; she has chosen to take up the line of being eccentric, and if she marries at all, I suppose she will marry somebody who likes that sort of thing. But you, my dear, are a very different kind of person, I am thankful to say, and you do yourself harm when you disregard the conventionalities."

This mild lecture, which was prolonged, with occasional breaks, until South Audley Street was reached, engrossed Veronica's attention just enough to keep the tears out of her eyes, and a letter, addressed in a straggling, schoolboy hand, which she found on her entrance, served the same desirable purpose. It was delightful to hear from Joe again, and still more delightful to learn, after the envelope had been torn open, that he was at home for a holiday.

"The man with whom I have been living in Lincolnshire has got a couple of children down with the measles," Joe wrote, "so I have been packed off, lest my precious life should be endangered. I am having a fairly good time of it at the old place, but it isn't a bit like home without you. Why don't you run down for a little and refresh yourself with a dose of rustic simplicity, like Virgil and Horace and other great poets, including the melodious Mostyn, who tells us that you are not yet wedded to town life? As I have often assured you, my dear, you would be wedded to me, if only I were a year or two older, and, after all, I don't know why we should let a mere question of age stand in our way. Think it over before you commit yourself to some other Johnny of less unimpeachable character. Anyhow, return for a time to your faithful and disconsolate—JOE.

"P.S.—I am walking a foxhound puppy—a perfect beauty. It would be well worth your while to come down here, if only to see him."

"I will!" exclaimed Veronica, who had perused the above epistle in the seclusion of her bedroom. "I know they will be glad to have me, and I shall be more than glad to get away from this."

Without more ado she marched downstairs and announced her intention of returning to Harbury Vale forthwith. "I want a change," she informed her astonished aunt; "all my business transactions with Mr. Walton have been brought to an end long ago, and it doesn't seem to be necessary that I should enter into possession of Broxham yet awhile. So I have made up my mind to forget for six weeks or a couple of months that I am a squiress, with all sorts of disagreeable responsibilities upon my shoulders. You can remind me of them when we meet again, later in the year."

Mrs. Mansfield could elicit nothing further than that from her; she had seen enough of London for the present; she wanted to go back to the country, and to the country she meant to go. It was all very well to say that in days gone by young people did not take up so peremptory a tone, and to point out that it is scarcely respectful to a duly consti-tuted duenna to form plans without even consulting her. But what, after all, is to be done with a lady who is of age, who is her own mistress and who proposes to take her own way? Veronica was con-ciliatory, grateful and affectionate, but firm: there was evidently nothing for it but to let her go, to be thankful for her assurance that she looked forward to welcoming Horace to his old home in September and to congratulate one's self upon being free to resume the course of one's own quiet, comfortable little existence during the summer months.

"I must say that you are very upsetting," Mrs. Mansfield felt it due to herself to remark. "Still, I suppose Mr. and Mrs. Dimsdale may be trusted to take care of you until the autumn, and, as I shall not be wanted, I think I will go to Marienbad and Switzerland." And to herself she added: "It will do Horace no harm to be shown that he isn't indispensable. Perhaps, too, it is just as well, upon the whole, that the engagement should not appear to have been brought about with too much precipitation. Of course her going off in a·hurry like this only means that they have had another small squabble."

CHAPTER XII.

HORACE CUTS A POOR FIGURE.

HORACE TREVOR, as he walked away from Lady Louisa Cradock's after that unlucky encounter with Verónica, was a seriously mortified young man. He could imagine so well what Veronica must be thinking of him! In fact, she had shown pretty plainly what she thought by taking no direct notice of him,. and by her disdainful remark that he was probably eager to be regaled with the conclusion of a scandalous anecdote. And really he had done nothing to merit her displeasure or contempt; on the contrary, he had, as it seemed to him, behaved as an honourable man from first to last. He had not wanted to fall in love with her; he had done what in him lay to conceal from her the fact that that misfortune had befallen him; he had agreed with her that the subject should be ignored

between them thenceforth and for ever. Why was
he to be scorned instead of pitied? Certainly he
could have wished that she had not found him
smoking and laughing in Dolly Cradock's sanctum,
and he had been aware of not looking particularly
like a disconsolate lover at the moment; but she
did not want him to look like a disconsolate lover,
he supposed. At least if she did, it was rather
unreasonable of her.

All this Horace said to himself with a view to
recovering the cheerful countenance of which he
had been deprived; but it did not help him very
much towards that desirable end. Of course, he
had a right to choose his own company and amuse
himself in his own way; but the distressing part
of it was that Veronica had for some time been
striving to inoculate him with a taste for better
company and more refined amusements, that he
had shown himself an apt disciple, and that he had
reverted to former habits immediately on discover-
ing that she had no notion of ever being anything
more than his friend. Naturally, her conclusion
would be that he had been deceiving her all along.
At the same time, it was too bad of her to have
jumped to such erroneous conclusions, however

natural they might be. Thus the downcast cogi-
tator wandered from one cause of complaint to
another; and the upshot of them all was that he
was a confoundedly unlucky fellow, that he wished
to goodness that he had never set eyes on Veronica
Dimsdale and that he would go out to Colorado,
or whatever the name of the beastly place was, and
be a cowboy—hanged if he wouldn't!

In this very fractious mood he remained for
several days, during which he took care to see no
friends, save those of his own sex, and was far from
civil even to them. But it was difficult to be surly
with Lord Chippenham, who hailed him, one afternoon, in Pall Mall, and for whom an ex-cavalry
lieutenant could not help retaining a respect akin to
that which schoolboys who have grown bald or gray-
headed always feel for a former head-master. So
when the General hooked him by the arm, saying,
"Walk down with me as far as Westminster, my
boy; I've got to go and record my vote against that
crew of Radical wiseacres that calls itself a Government," there was nothing for it but to comply with
a good grace, although what was coming might be
guessed in advance. Lord Chippenham led his
captive past the Duke of York's column and down

the steps into the Mall, discoursing upon the defenceless state of these islands, and then attacked a question of more pressing personal interest.

"I don't see the good of shilly-shallying," he declared, "and I tell you plainly, my dear fellow, that to my mind you are behaving almost as much like an ass as the Prime Minister. Julia Mansfield may say what she likes, but when a thing has to be done, the sooner it's done the better; who knows what may happen while you stand shivering on the brink? Why haven't you proposed to that girl yet, eh?"

"Well, I don't know that it is one of the things that have got to be done," answered Horace; "in point of fact, I should say that it was one of the things which are precious unlikely to be done."

"Don't talk such nonsense! Haven't I been watching you both for weeks?—and was I born yesterday? It's very evident to me that you have fallen in love with the girl—and a devilish sensible thing to do too! Now, how long do you imagine that you will be allowed to go on dancing attendance upon her without speaking out? How long——"

"But I'm not dancing attendance upon her," interrupted Horace.

"You have been, anyhow; you won't deny that, I suppose. There's such a thing as letting one's opportunity slip, and there are plenty of men who ask nothing better than to take your place, let me tell you, young fellow. Come, now! Be a man or a mouse. What are you afraid of? If you have taken it into your head that she is likely to refuse you, you have taken an uncommonly silly notion into your head; I don't mind saying as much as that to you."

Horace thought for a moment of mentioning the reasons which must always render it impossible for him to offer marriage to the heiress of the late Mr. Trevor, but he decided to spare himself the nuisance of an unprofitable discussion, and only remarked that he was not so cocksure of success as all that.

"Well, hang it all, man! you can but try," returned Lord Chippenham. "If you fail, you will fail, and there will be no more to be said; but I shall have a poor opinion of you if you let Miss Veronica leave London without having had the chance of saying whether she wishes to accept you or not."

All the rest of the way to the House of Lords he enlarged upon the folly of quarrelling with your bread and butter in a style most exasperating to his hearer, who at length exclaimed—

"Very well, then! If I propose and get my answer—which will be No—perhaps you and Aunt Julia won't bother me any more about the matter."

He really did, in his wrath and irritation, intend to carry out that crazy project. After all, why not? Veronica already knew all that there was to know and already despised him. The mere fact of having to repeat what she had said before, in answer to a formal proposition which had not been made before, would hardly trouble her, while it would free him from the importunities of officious relatives. Moreover, he was in one of those naughty tempers which make us childishly anxious to seek the deepest depths of humiliation. "You despise me, do you?" he was saying to himself, in effect. "All right, then, you shall have something to despise me for."

Off he went, therefore, to South Audley Street, with a quick, resolute step, and although his heart may have sunk a little as he ascended the well-known staircase in the wake of the butler, he promised himself that he would not leave the house before he should have received the slap in the face which he courted.

"This," remarked Mrs. Mansfield, rising and holding out her hand to him, "is a kindly act which I scarcely ventured to hope for. I had made up my mind that I should see no more of you now that Veronica has left me."

"Veronica left you!" ejaculated the young man; "you don't mean to say so! Has she gone for good then?"

"Well, she doesn't return to me until the autumn, when I am to chaperon her at Broxham, I believe. For the present she has gone to her uncle and aunt at Harbury Vale. I thought you knew."

"No," answered Horace slowly, as he dropped into a chair, "this is the first I have heard of it. Wasn't it rather a sudden move on her part?"

"Yes, rather; but she is a sudden sort of person. I dare say you may have noticed that."

Horace made no rejoinder. His sensation was in reality one of immense relief, but he looked sufficiently dismayed to satisfy Mrs. Mansfield, who took a malicious pleasure in his apparent consternation. She judged it appropriate to remark: "Veronica has an old head upon young shoulders; it hasn't been in the least turned by her change of fortune or by the admiration of which, as you know, she has had a good deal. Or, perhaps, you don't know, for we have seen so little of you lately. Next season, when she will be out of mourning and will have grown accustomed to her position, no doubt she will have an even larger selection of suitors to choose from. I shouldn't be at all surprised if she has left London now just because she is not quite prepared to make her choice yet."

"Ah! very likely," said Horace abstractedly.

He was wondering within himself what Veronica's real reason could have been for vanishing away without a word of farewell. He did not flatter himself that she cared enough for his friendship to have gone off in a huff; yet she would surely have wished him good-bye if she had not meant him to understand that he was in her black books.

"I wonder at her not having told you she was going. I supposed that she had at least written you a note," Mrs. Mansfield remarked placidly. "You have been such good friends all along, in spite of her having, in a sense, robbed you; and it has been such a pleasure to me to see your intimacy."

"She has not robbed me in any sense whatever," returned Horace, a little tartly. "As for friendship, well, as you told me at the first, of course she isn't at all my style, and we were hardly likely to develop into bosom friends when it came to be a question of intimacy. Not that I don't like her very much, and I am sorry that it will be another twelve months before I see her again—that is, if I am still in England twelve months hence."

"My dear boy!" exclaimed Mrs. Mansfield, rather alarmed by this veiled threat, "what are you talking about? You surely don't contemplate emigrating or doing anything insane of that sort! And you will certainly see Veronica again in September. She counts upon you to come to Broxham for the partridge-shooting, and so do I. I should never forgive you if you were to leave us in the lurch. Just think of it! Shooting-parties there must be; and how are two helpless women to make them go off without assistance?"

Horace laughed. "Look here, Aunt Julia," said he; "I know perfectly well what you are driving at, and I have known it ever since you began to play the game. In fact, I may as well tell you that I was sent here by the General this afternoon for the express purpose of proposing to Veronica. She would have refused me, of course, and I thought that, after that, you and he would leave us in peace.

Now, I do want you to understand quite clearly that she would never, under any circumstances, consent to marry me. Unless that much is understood I would rather be shot myself than help your friends to shoot the Broxham partridges. Will you take my word for it that the match is out of the question ?"

Mrs. Mansfield was by no means a stupid woman, but she was scarcely clever enough to feel certain of the response which she was expected to make to this appeal. What she thought it, upon the whole, best to say (in view of the paramount importance of securing her nephew's presence at Broxham in the autumn) was: " Horace, I will be honest with you. I did very much wish and hope that Veronica might take a fancy to you: you must admit that it would have been a most fortunate thing on all grounds if she had. Still, as you are so sure that it can't be, I won't worry you any more about it—and, indeed, I have always been afraid that you were not quite intellectual enough to please her. Never mind! What can't be cured must be endured. Come to Broxham as her friend—or rather as her cousin— and I can promise you, on her behalf, that you shall have the warmest of welcomes."

Nothing could well have been more satisfactory than the young man's reply. He said he should be glad to be welcomed on those terms. He added that, knowing the place so well, he might probably be of some use to Veronica and her guests, and he looked as crestfallen as his aunt could have wished. Nevertheless, from Mrs. Mansfield's point of view, there had been some lack of prudence in taking him so promptly at his word. Had his sentiments been those which were not unnaturally imputed to him, a snub would doubtless have served its purpose; but since he had not the faintest intention of ever asking the heiress to be his wife, that allusion to his intellectual inferiority was a little unfortunate. It caused him to say to himself, when he left South Audley Street, after promising to keep himself free from engagements until a date for his visit to Broxham could be fixed, that he had been a perfect fool to imagine that even friendship between him and the superior Veronica was a possible thing; it caused him to suspect that she must have laughed at his innocent endeavours to educate himself up to her level and to resolve that there should be no renewal of such endeavours. It likewise caused him to reflect that in friendship as well as in love there must be some sort of equality between the parties and that the Dolly Cradocks of this world were much more in his line than the Veronica Dimsdales. If Dolly had had a thousand a year of her own the chances are that he would have proceeded straightway to place his hand and heart at her disposal, by way of proving his sense of the general fitness of things.

Dolly having nothing of her own, and having never made any secret of the fact that her future husband must be a wealthy man, he was preserved from doing anything quite so silly as that; but he solaced himself by frequenting resorts where he was pretty sure of meeting her, and he was downright sentimental in the language which he employed when—as not unfrequently happened—he and she were left to say to one another what nobody else could overhear. Now, Dolly, whatever may have been her failings, was assuredly not a sentimental person; she fully recognised that there is all the difference in the world between the poetry of love and the prose of matrimony, and although Horace Trevor, with the Broxham estate and £100,000 or so invested in safe securities, would have suited her well enough, she had no more

notion of espousing the actual Horace than of
taking a flying leap from the parapet of Westminster Bridge. Yet it is not necessary to have a
hard heart because one is blessed with a clear, sane
understanding, nor was there any reason at all why
the young man's quasi-amorous speeches should not
sound very pleasantly in her ears. She believed
that he was genuinely in love with her, which is
always an agreeable sort of belief to entertain and
was in her case justified by the circumstance that
a great many other impecunious young men were,
or professed to be, in the same sad predicament.
Moreover, he had as good as told her that he was.

Thus it came to pass, after a time, that the soft
influences of a moonlight night—supplemented, it
may be, by those of a good dinner and excellent
champagne—brought about a scene between this
pair which had better not have taken place. They
had been dining with a large party at one of those
river-side club-houses which have sprung up of late
years, and the gardens of which may have witnessed
more than one scene equally undesirable from the
subsequent point of view of the persons concerned
therein ; they had wandered away from their
friends, they were contemplating the broad, silent

stream, and they had been lamenting, as it was extremely natural to do, that following up the bright track shed upon it by the full moon would never lead them to the traditional pot of gold of which they both stood so much in need.

"What would you do with it if you got it?" Dolly asked. "I don't mean a wretched little pipkin, containing twenty spade-guineas, or anything of that sort, but a good solid fortune of, say, half a million?"

"I should give it to you," answered Horace, without hesitation.

"What, unconditionally? I don't for one moment believe that you would; but I can assure you that, if you did, you would never see a single penny of it back again."

"Oh, well, there would be conditions attached to the gift, of course—one condition, at least. You would have to take me with it."

Dolly Cradock was really an extremely handsome girl, and just then she was looking her very best. At the moment he spoke he was almost, if not quite, sincere.

"Ah," she answered, with a touch of bitterness, "that is a mere detail. Everybody who knows me knows that I should take a hunchback or a cripple who had half a million of money to offer me. Beggars mustn't be choosers."

" But supposing that you weren't a beggar, and supposing that you *could* choose ?" Horace asked, drawing a little nearer to her.

" That's quite another question ; I don't see why I should answer it."

" I don't see why you shouldn't ; we are quite alone, and I am not very likely to repeat anything you may tell me, Dolly."

" Not to the blameless Veronica ?"

" Why to her, of all people in the world ?"

" Only because, a few weeks ago, you were thinking seriously of marrying her, and because in all probability you will be thinking of it seriously again a few weeks hence."

" I never thought, seriously or otherwise, of doing any such thing !" Horace declared indignantly.

" Oh, yes, you did ; *I* don't blame you. As I said just now, beggars mustn't be choosers, and I myself am bound to be as mercenary as you. As a rule, I feel tolerably resigned to my fate—and so do you, I suspect," added Dolly, with a half-smothered sigh.

Is it necessary to record what happened next? Eavesdropping is an ignoble occupation, and if it be our ill-fortune to surprise any two of our acquaintances in a compromising attitude, we instinctively turn and flee. Everything leads the present narrator to believe that Miss Dolly Cradock had been kissed by gentlemen who had no sort of excuse for thus saluting her before that evening when Horace Trevor was betrayed into saying things which he did not really mean, and it may be safely assumed that her indiscretions weighed lightly upon her conscience; but there is no need to dwell upon an episode in which the hero of this story cuts a poor figure, and we may pass on to the words of unexceptionable wisdom with which the interview was brought to a close.

" Now we won't play the fool any more," Dolly said briskly; " I'm sorry for you, and perhaps a little bit sorry for myself too ; but we shall both of us be all right again in a day or two, if not sooner. This has been merely a pretty little *intermezzo*, if you please ; it is not to have any consequences, and it is to be forgotten with all possible despatch. Go and see whether they aren't putting the horses in."

Horace had been saying things which he did not

mean ; but Dolly, to do her justice, seldom erred in that way. Shortly afterwards she took her place upon the box-seat of the drag which was to convey them back to London and was driven by an elderly widower of large means, to whom she made herself most agreeable. Horace listened to her wonderingly, while tardy repentance and shame gained the mastery over him. Put it how he would, he could not but feel that he had disgraced himself. He did not love Dolly ; he did not in his heart believe that she cared a brass farthing for him ; and although Veronica would never know that he had been false to her, and would also not care a brass farthing if she did, the fact that he had been false remained. " It's time for me to be off," was his conclusion. " I really can't look that girl in the face again to-morrow, as if nothing had happened, though I expect she will be able to keep her countenance easily enough. I shall go to Ireland and fish."

CHAPTER XIII.

"At the present moment," remarked Veronica lazily, "I am perfectly happy, comfortable and contented. I wonder how many other people there are now in this country who could say the same thing— or would, if they could!"

"The population of the United Kingdom is, I believe, thirty-eight millions odd," answered Joe. "Probably we shall be making a liberal allowance if we estimate that twenty persons out of the lot are as highly blessed as you are and have the decency to acknowledge it. Sorry I can't include my own name in the select band, but a *proxime accessit* is as much as I feel justified in allowing myself. I want but little here below, only I want just a little bit more than I have got."

The boat in which they were seated lay motionless

and half hidden by tall rushes in a quiet backwater of the river; overhead the August sun was blazing out of a cloudless sky. Veronica, reclining beneath a white sunshade upon a pile of cushions, was enjoying that delight in mere existence and absolute idleness which is so seldom granted to us northern islanders, while her cousin, clad in flannels, with his sleeves rolled up and his elbows upon his knees, was placidly smoking the short pipe which was rather more often between his lips than it ought to have been at his age.

Veronica laughed. "What makes you such a thoroughly satisfactory companion, Joseph," said she, "is that you are so unsophisticated. Now, if you had been mixing in good society ever since the spring, as I have, you would have felt it simply imperative upon you to swear that the actual situation was a sort of foretaste of Paradise."

"Do you suppose that anything would make me talk such rot as that to *you* ?" asked Joe disgustedly. "If you want to be flattered and humbugged you had better send for some of your smart London friends, or telegraph for old Mostyn, who always has a large surplus stock of sugary speeches on hand. From me, my beloved Veronica, you will never hear anything but the truth ; and the truth is that I am jolly glad to be sitting here and talking to you again."

" Well, didn't I tell you that you were satisfactory ?   Only I wish you hadn't said that you wanted more than you had got, because that reminds me of the quantity of things which I want and am not at all likely to get—and my object was to put them out of mind for the time being."

Joe shook his head. " I fear, Veronica," said he, " that you did not profit as you might have done by last Sunday's discourse.   In all my experience I have never met with anyone who preached the duty of taking things easy more persistently than the rector of this parish, and I may add that I have seldom met anyone who practised it less.   However, that is neither here nor there.   What are all these things that you want so badly, if one may ask ?"

" Perhaps I ought rather to have said that there are things of which I want to get rid," answered Veronica ; "but never mind. I am rid of them temporarily, at all events."

" Now, look here, my dear girl," said Joe impressively, " don't you go ridding yourself of your landed

estates, whatever you do. Think of others. Think
of me, for example, and of the bitter disappointment
that it would be to me to be debarred from shooting
your coverts when the time comes. I have nothing
to say against a compromise, mind you ; I have told
you, ever since you came back and I heard your
account of that chap Trevor, that in my opinion you
couldn't bestow your affections more worthily than
upon him. Then you would feel that you had
behaved handsomely, the property would be his as
well as yours and everybody would be pleased.
Because I don't think so meanly of you as to imagine
that you would ever consent to become his wife
without stipulating that I should be invited to Broxham whenever there was a big shoot on."

This time Veronica did not laugh. " Unfortunately, that compromise is out of the question,"
she said ; " Horace Trevor and I are quite of one
mind as to the impossibility of it."

" Oh, you have talked it over together, then ?"

" Yes, we talked it over, and we agreed that our
mutual liking was not of the kind that could be
made to do. Besides, there are other obstacles.
I don't know how I am to manage matters so as to
do the best that I can for you all, and you have

completely destroyed my comfort by introducing the horrid subject. Pull me down stream again and let us talk about something else—foxes or badgers, or what you please. Wasn't it to the badgers' earths that you and Nipper went off before breakfast this morning?"

Joe had plenty to say upon that engrossing topic, and was quite willing to comply with Veronica's request. He never forced her confidences, being well aware that she generally ended by telling him almost everything, and having a much more real sympathy with her perplexities than his speech betrayed. She, on her side, knew that she could rely upon his comprehension and sympathy, but she also knew that Joe had too much common-sense to approve of her despoiling herself of her inheritance in favour of Dolly Cradock, and that was why she had not mentioned Dolly's name to him. Indeed, as she had avowed, her one great wish was to forget for a while the complex burdens which had come upon her together with what every-body still persisted in calling her extraordinary good luck. She would have to take them up again soon ; during those few weeks of summer she desired to ignore them and to revert to the old days when she had been less envied and a good deal less unenviable.

But to put the clock back is a feat which has never yet been accomplished by man or woman with any perceptible effect upon the passage of time, and although Veronica tried very hard to persuade herself that she was unchanged, her uncle and aunt were always at hand to point out to her what a fallacy that was. They were kindness itself to her, those good people, and they had also—after some protest—allowed her to be kind to them in a pecuniary sense, which was a comfort so far as it went. But it would have been worse than useless even to hint in their hearing at her fixed determination to resign the estate which had been bequeathed to her, and it was always rather a sore point with Veronica that they were willing to acquiesce with such alacrity in her departure from the home of her childhood.

"Well, you see, my dear," Mrs. Dimsdale said, in answer to some tentative reproaches which were addressed to her on that score, "it is very much the same thing as if you were going to be married, and naturally I have always hoped that you would marry. I am sure I have felt it as a horrid wrench when our own girls have left us; still, one knows that it is what Providence intended them to do and that children can't be children for ever. One thinks of their happiness, not of one's own."

"Only the difference between them and me is that I am not going to be married," objected Veronica.

"Oh, you are going to be married," returned her aunt, laughing. "Perhaps, if you were to make a point of it, I could even tell you the name of the man whom you are going to marry."

That closed Veronica's lips and the conversation. The unanimity with which all who took an interest in her had decided that it was her manifest destiny to become Mrs. Horace Trevor almost made her wish that Horace himself was less obstinately recalcitrant. The only dissentient voice had been that of Mr. Mostyn, and the moral support of Mr. Mostyn was not just then available, the poet having crossed the Channel to refresh himself by communings with French men of letters, among whom he was highly esteemed. Harbury Vale, therefore, was not what it had been in days of yore, nor could all the making-believe in the world render it so; and when Joe left for Lincolnshire, in order to obtain practical experience of harvesting operations, Veronica was not disinclined to bring her own holiday to an end.

It turned out, however, that her new home could not be prepared for her reception at quite so early a date as had been anticipated. Mrs. Mansfield, who was already at Broxham, and who had most kindly undertaken the management of all necessary details, wrote to say that there was still a great deal to be done, and that the partridges would have to remain unmolested, she feared, until the end of September. "Of course, I shall be delighted to have you with me, dear, if you care to come at once; but I am afraid it would be dreadfully dull for you, because we can't ask people to stay until the bed-rooms have been made tidy. Poor dear Samuel lived so much alone latterly, and I have been obliged to dismiss the housekeeper, who had become so rude and independent that I am sure you would never have been able to stand her. As for Horace, he has had an invitation to a Scotch deer-forest, which he says he could not resist; but he promises to be with us for the first of the covert-shooting. So please do as you like about coming here; only don't think yourself bound to lend me a hand, for, troublesome as it is, I can do very well without help, and I should like you to have a more pleasant first impression of the place than you would get if you were to see it in its present dismantled condition."

Veronica rightly interpreted this as meaning that Mrs. Mansfield was revelling in the choice of upholstery and did not wish to be interfered with. Accordingly, she remained where she was, being made heartily welcome to do so, although her aunt Elizabeth could not help expressing some surprise at her indifference respecting a very important matter.

"I really do think I should want to see my own furniture before I bought it—not to speak of engaging my own servants!" the good lady exclaimed.

But Veronica knew that neither furniture nor servants would be hers for long, and her wish was to shorten as far as might be the prelude to the pre-arranged domestic drama. She had rehearsed it all in advance—Horace's arrival, which must be speedily followed by that of Dolly Cradock; the opportunities that were to be given them for coming to a mutual understanding, the temporary despondency of the lovers, and then her own more or less graceful retirement. With a little management success ought to be her reward; but she was impatient to begin, and it would be time enough for her to step upon the stage when the curtain should be ready to rise.

It was through a curtain of mist and rain that her eyes at length beheld the large and substantial, but not very imposing mansion of which she was the mistress. A solid, stone-coloured house, with a Greek portico and a number of bow windows, encircled by a rather meagre flower-garden, standing in the midst of a level park, where there were some fine trees, and hemmed in on all sides by distant woods—this was what she saw as she was driven rapidly from the station in the carriage which had been sent to meet her on that stormy autumn evening, and she said to herself that she would, at least, be able to resign that residence without a single pang of regret. It was not in the least beautiful, and it did not look like the sort of place to which one could ever become much attached. However, when the carriage drew up at the door, and she was admitted into a spacious, well-lighted hall, where a cheerful wood-fire was blazing, and where busts, tall Oriental vases, Persian rugs and Japanese screens had been arranged in an artistic fashion, she had to admit that Broxham was a good deal more attractive within than without. And the affectionate embrace of Aunt Julia, who came out to greet her, followed by Lord Chippenham, was pleasanter than the respectful, furtive scrutiny of the butler and the footman, who relieved her of her wraps. Perhaps the servants regarded Mrs. Mansfield, who had engaged them, as their mistress, rather than the young lady from whom they had been told they were in future to take their orders ; and certainly Mrs. Mansfield appeared to have made herself very much at home, having, as she presently informed Veronica, invited one or two people, besides Lord Chippenham, "just to keep the place warm for you."

"I hope you don't mind, dear," she added. "You won't find any of them at all troublesome to entertain."

Veronica did not mind in the least; on the contrary, she was extremely grateful to her aunt for having so ably replaced her, and she expressed her gratitude while she was being led into a comfortable

library where half-a-dozen ladies and a couple of
young men were grouped round the tea-table.

" Oh, I have done nothing," declared Mrs. Mansfield, who nevertheless thought that she deserved
some thanks. " I have only got rid of some of
poor Samuel's impossible old retainers, who had
already been fully provided for in his will and who
didn't care to stay. And I have pulled the furniture
about and spent a little of your money—that is all.
I think you will find everything in tolerably good
order, and now that you have come, I am delighted
to surrender the reins of government to you."

But it soon became evident that that surrender
would be far from delightful to her; nor was she
called upon to make it, save nominally. Veronica
sat at the head of the table and held a long obliga-
tory conference with the agent and the bailiff on
the following morning; but it was Mrs. Mansfield
who saw the housekeeper after breakfast and drew
up the programme for the day. She said : " Perhaps
I had better continue to look after things for you
until you have shaken down into your place," and
she was assured that the longer she was kind
enough to do so the better her niece would be
pleased.

It is not certain that Veronica, who had clear
ideas of the duties belonging to every station of
life, would have been equally complaisant had she
looked upon herself as being in any real sense the
proprietress of the Broxham estate; but since she
meant to turn her back upon it at the earliest possible opportunity she was only too glad to make
Aunt Julia happy by self-effacement.   Meanwhile,
she had a pleasant enough time of it for the next
ten days.   The house, if not magnificent, was comfortable and home-like; there was a charming old
walled garden within easy reach of it where one
could wander and explore without being thought
neglectful of one's guests; Aunt Julia's friends, of
whom several relays arrived and left during the
above-mentioned period, were very nice easy-going
sort of people, who rose late in the morning, seemed
to be satisfied with a drive in the afternoon, and
entertained one another.   As for the men, they were
out shooting all day long; Lord Chippenham took
charge of them pending the advent of Horace, who
was expected to make his appearance from Scotland
shortly.   That Horace, when he came, would act
as the *de facto* master of the establishment was
evidently taken for granted by its inmates, both

permanent and temporary. Indeed, so far as grooms, gamekeepers, beaters and other outdoor dependents were concerned, he had, it seemed, acted in that capacity for some years past.

He arrived late one evening, looking very well and sunburnt, and Veronica noticed at once, with great satisfaction, that he had discarded the embarrassed and somewhat sullen manner which had provoked her during the latter part of her sojourn in London. This she took as a sign that he had now realised the absurdity of the misgivings as to which he had then pleaded guilty, and that he was ready to meet her once more upon the old friendly footing. Such was, in truth, his laudable intention and desire. Months of fresh air and hard exercise had done so much for him that he was able by this time, as he believed, to put a good face upon unalterable facts. Veronica most certainly was not for him; he had been a deplorable idiot to fall in love with her and a still greater idiot to let her discover his idiocy; but he had now come to his senses, and he hoped to make it quite clear to her that her friendship was all that he asked. Of Dolly Cradock and the circumstances under which he had parted from her it has to be confessed that he had thought very

little indeed in the course of an enjoyable summer
and autumn. It is the destiny of these light-hearted
young ladies to be forgotten as readily as they are
wont to forget, and had not she herself said that
an episode upon which it was not altogether
pleasant to look back was to have no consequences?

"And what have you been doing all this long
time?" Veronica wanted to know, when he crossed
the long drawing-room to seat himself beside her
after dinner on the evening of his arrival.

"Well," he answered, "I expect you would say
that I have been doing nothing. I have been
yachting a little, and I have been fishing and shooting. That's what you call sheer waste of time, isn't
it?"

"I don't know; it just depends upon whether
there was any better use for you to make of your
time, and I should hardly think that there was.
Besides, I have been absolutely idle myself; so that
it doesn't become me to condemn my neighbours."

"I should have thought you would have been as
busy as a bee," said Horace, looking admiringly
round him. "You have beautified this old barrack
out of all recognition. How do you like the place,
now that you have taken possession of it?"

"Oh, pretty well," answered Veronica, "but the beautifying has been Aunt Julia's work, and of course Broxham can never seem like home to me. I have no associations with it, as you have. You will find any number of humble friends eager to welcome you to-morrow, and I do hope that, in charity to me, you mean to stay a long time. I have already had to promise faithfully that you will hunt from here this season."

Horace laughed and made a grimace. "I shall have to explain to these good folks that times have changed, I see," said he. "I'll stay a week or two for the covert shooting, if you'll have me; but as for hunting, that's another affair. To begin with, I haven't anything to ride."

"I was to tell you that every care has been taken of the dun horse and the little bay, and that they are both of them in first-rate condition."

"Glad to hear it; but they are your horses, not mine, remember."

"That doesn't seem to be the general opinion. Uncle Samuel bought them for you, I am told; and even if they are legally my property, they are of about as much use to me as a pair of giraffes would be. So please take them away, if you want to take them away, though we shall all feel rather hurt by your choosing to hunt in another country."

Horace could not afford to hunt in any country; but he did not want to keep on alluding to his poverty, and, as a matter of fact, the temptation held out to him was a very hard one to resist. Therefore, he only said, after a pause, "But I can't *live* here, you know, Veronica."

"But you can stay here sometimes, as you used to do," she returned. "You have only to substitute me—or rather, Aunt Julia—for Uncle Samuel, and from all that I hear, the change will be a change for the better in some respects."

Horace did not contradict her. Later, it would no doubt be necessary to explain that he could not accept such unbounded hospitality; but for the moment he was unwilling to make difficulties. Besides, to tell the truth, he did think that it would be rather jolly to have just three or four more days with the old hounds.

So all this was as satisfactory as possible, and it only remained to summon Dolly Cradock forthwith.

END OF VOL. I.

BILLING AND SONS, PRINTERS, GUILDFORD.